Our eyes met. For a moment my breath caught in my throat. "Well," I said quickly, starting to rise. "I'd better be going...."

"What's your hurry?" Josh took my arm and held it.

"Bitsy's expecting me."

"She won't be worried. She knows you're with me. I wanted to see you tonight."

"I can't. I told Bitsy I'd—"

"I dare you," Josh said softly.

"You've done that to me before, Josh Connelly."

"Yes, I have. And as I recall, it worked out okay. Since this is the second time, I guess maybe I ought to double dare you."

"All right." I grinned at him. "What is it this time?"

Josh's smile was slow and satisfied. "I dare you not to keep running away from me, Ali."

Dear Readers:

Thank you for your unflagging interest in First Love From Silhouette. Your many helpful letters have shown us that you have appreciated growing and stretching with us, and that you demand more from your reading than happy endings and conventional love stories. In the months to come we will make sure that our stories go on providing the variety you have come to expect from us. We think you will enjoy our unusual plot twists and unpredictable characters who will surprise and delight you without straying too far from the concerns that are very much part of all our daily lives.

We hope you will continue to share with us your ideas about how to keep our books your very First Loves. We depend on you to keep us on our toes!

Nancy Jackson
Senior Editor
FIRST LOVE FROM SILHOUETTE

DOUBLE DARE
Laurien Berenson

First Love from Silhouette

Published by Silhouette Books New York

America's Publisher of Contemporary Romance

SILHOUETTE BOOKS
300 E. 42nd St., New York, N.Y. 10017

Copyright © 1986 by Laurien Berenson

ISBN: 0-373-06208-7

First Silhouette Books printing October 1986

America's Publisher of Contemporary Romance

Printed in the U.S.A.

RL 5.0, IL age 10 and up

LAURIEN BERENSON loves all sports. She is especially fond of tennis and, as readers of *Double Dare* may have guessed, horseback riding. As a teenager, she was a nationally ranked rider. Ms. Berenson also enjoys breeding and showing miniature poodles. An enthusiastic traveler, she has visited every state in the Union from Alaska to Florida. She now lives in Connecticut with her husband and son.

Chapter One

Usually I'm not at all the sort of person who likes to take foolish chances. In fact, just the opposite is true. My brother, Pete, who's a year younger than I am but thinks he knows everything, says that when I was born they must have mixed up the babies in the hospital nursery, otherwise I never would have ended up in our family at all. Then again, his idea of a good time is diving, headfirst, off a twenty-foot cliff into a tiny pool of water, so how much could he possibly know?

All of which does nothing to explain how it was that I happened to find myself on the back of a small, chestnut Thoroughbred in the main ring at the Ox Ridge Horse Show, facing a course of fences that were higher than his head and mine put together. Of course the fact that he was my horse, and that his name was Dare Me, might have had something to do with it. Still, I had no business being out there in the middle of a jumper class at all.

The problem was, I never should have listened to Tommy Meehan in the first place. He's always mouthing off about something or other. Unfortunately I have what might be called a quick temper. My mother tells me that it comes from having red hair, and since she has them both, too, I guess she ought to know. Anyway, Tommy always seems to know just what will make me mad. Either that or he really is every bit as dumb as his idiotic comments make him sound.

Of course Tommy, who wouldn't know what finesse was if it came up and shook his hand, competes in the jumper division with his horse, Lobo. This morning he'd had the nerve to say that most horses are shown in the hunter class because they didn't have the talent to handle the big fences. Somebody had to prove him wrong. When Josh Connelly, his equally smart-mouthed friend agreed, I knew that someone was going to be me.

Dare Me's ears pricked forward as he measured the size of the fence before us. He slowed uncertainly. Shifting my weight forward, I urged him to gallop on. Reassured, he responded with all the game determination that was his Thoroughbred heritage.

He could do it. The fences were higher than he was used to, but not impossible. Besides, Dare Me was the kind of horse who gave you everything you asked of him, or broke his heart trying. If any of the hunters could make it around the jumper course and force Tommy and Josh to eat their words, he was the one.

Feeling suddenly rather pleased with myself, I pictured how much I was going to enjoy the looks on their faces when they found they'd been shown up. Then we reached the first fence, and I forgot everything but riding the course. Gathering himself onto his haunches, Dare Me sprang into the air with a mighty leap. For a moment I was thrown by the sheer power of his thrust. Then quickly I righted myself, concentrating on using my weight to his best advantage.

There now, I thought as we landed on the far side. That wasn't so bad, was it?

One by one, the fences came and Dare Me, bless him, handled them all with the same aplomb. The wall, the spread, the triple bar, all flashed by in quick succession as Dare Me flew over the course as though he'd been born to it. Finally I swung him wide on the last turn to face the only fence that remained.

The water jump, I thought with a sudden, sinking feeling. I'd forgotten all about it! Horses, by nature, seem to have a thing about jumping over water. Dare Me, as I recalled from the puddles and streams we'd come across while out hacking, was no exception.

Sitting back in the saddle, I steeled myself for the conflict that was sure to come. Though usually very accommodating as Thoroughbreds went, when Dare Me didn't like something, he had no compunction about making his feelings known. His nostrils flared as he picked up the approaching scent. From the way his back humped beneath the saddle, I knew right away I was in for trouble.

By now, however, success was so close I could almost taste it. Only one more fence lay between me and the victory I longed to savor. I had no intention of letting anything, even a thousand pounds of stubborn Thoroughbred, stand in my way. Taking a firmer grip on the reins, I sat back in the saddle, dug my heels and pushed. Dare Me resisted. I pushed harder.

All the way up to the final stride, the battle of wills continued. It wasn't until then, when I felt him gather himself for the takeoff, that I relaxed. That was my big mistake. In that final second before he left the ground, Dare Me changed his mind and chickened out.

Ducking to one side, he dropped his shoulder, a trick that is guaranteed to unseat all but the most attentive riders. I, with my thoughts already racing ahead to the gloating I planned to do shortly, didn't qualify. All I knew was that suddenly it felt as though the world had dropped out from underneath me. Where only moments before had been a long, chestnut neck, now there was only empty space. The hold I tried to find with my legs was too little, too late.

With the greatest of ease, I sailed out of the saddle, somersaulting through the air to land with a loud splash right in the middle of the shallow trough of water. Unhurt, I scrambled quickly to my feet. I was just in time to watch Dare Me gallop away across the ring, kicking up his heels defiantly as he went.

I sloshed my way out of the pool, shaking off the excess water like a wet puppy. I was wet clear through. My breeches were cold and clammy, and clung to my legs. My high, black leather boots squished when I walked. Beads of water dripped down off the brow of my velvet hard hat to land with annoying precision on the tip of my nose.

"Are you all right, miss?" The red-coated ringmaster hurried over, an anxious look on his face.

"Fine," I mumbled, managing a wan smile for reassurance, "More embarrassed than anything else."

That was certainly true, I thought as I waited for the jump crew to round up Dare Me from the far end of the ring and bring him back. What a fiasco this had turned out to be.

All too soon, Dare Me was returned, and the ringmaster gave me a leg up back into the saddle. Even though by falling off I had been eliminated from the class, it was courtesy to allow an exhibitor to school his horse over one last fence before leaving the ring. Quickly I popped the gelding over the triple bar, then pulled and trotted out the open gate.

My brother, Pete, was waiting for me outside. He was working for the Kingman stables this summer as a groom, which wasn't nearly as unfair an arrangement as it sounds. Though he liked horses enough, he'd never been particularly crazy about riding them, as I was. What he was crazy about though, was making money. Since there are only a limited number of ways a fifteen-year-old can do that, I guess he figured that grooming horses was as good a way as any.

Besides, this arrangement had the added bonus of giving us both more freedom than we'd ever be able to enjoy at home. The year before when I'd been on the circuit by myself, either one or the other of my parents traveled with me. This winter when I got my driver's license, I figured I'd finally be able to go by myself. Since the circuit winds its way all up and down the East Coast, however, my parents were somewhat hesitant about letting me simply take off on my own.

That's when Pete entered the picture. Talking in that low reassuring voice he uses whenever he wants Mom and Dad to think of him as a mature, responsible adult, he told them that he'd be happy to go along and chaperone me if it would make them feel any better. I'd have argued with that on principle except, to my surprise, it seemed to be working. I may not have agreed with his choice of words, but I sure knew better than to mess up a good thing when I heard it.

So here we were. In the three weeks since school let out, we'd been to Pennsylvania for the Devon show, and to Virginia for Upperville, before landing at the Ox Ridge Hunt Club in Connecticut the day before yesterday. Up to now, everything had been going great. Now if only my impossibly demanding coach Jack Kingman wasn't too mad.

Pete dashed that hope with his first words. "Are you ever in for it now," he said, taking my reins as I slid from the saddle. "Jack was here a minute ago, watching, and he's fit to be tied."

I scanned the crowd around us, but didn't see his bushy head of black hair anywhere. "Where'd he go?" I asked, thinking maybe I'd take the coward's way out and head off in the other direction.

"Beat's me." Pete shrugged. "Maybe back to the barn to get his horsewhip?"

"Thanks a lot," I said with a grimace. "You might try showing a little more brotherly concern, you know. Don't forget, if I get sent home from the circuit, you go with me."

Pete's teasing grin faded. "Yikes, you're right! I didn't even think about that." He busied himself with taking care of Dare Me, first running up the stirrups on either side of the saddle, then throwing a light, woven cooler over the gelding's back so that he wouldn't cool down too quickly after his exertion.

Watching Pete, I knew exactly what he was up to. Just because I was in trouble didn't mean that he was going to give Jack any excuse to come down hard on his case as well. One Anderson sibling in disgrace was enough for one afternoon.

I slipped off my riding jacket, shook out the excess water and draped it over my arm. It was going to need to be dry-cleaned and blocked before it could be worn again. And the sooner I got my boots off and their wooden boot trees into them the better off they'd be.

Pete led Dare Me away, back toward the temporary stabling that had been set up to accommodate the hundreds of horses that had come from all over the country to compete. Traveling at a much slower pace, I followed. No use in putting things off, I decided. Whatever Jack was going to do to me, I might as well get it over with.

No sooner had I left the chute than I was waylaid by Tommy and Josh. Both were looking inordinately pleased with themselves. If I'd hoped for sympathy, I knew I wasn't about to find it here.

"Hey," said Josh, flashing that wide grin that makes the dimple appear in his right cheek. "Great ride."

A compliment was the last thing I expected from him, and I looked up in surprise. For a moment as he stared at me with those big, dark brown eyes of his, I could have sworn that he was sincere.

Then Tommy chimed in from the other side. "Yeah," he crowed. "Great landing!"

"I'm glad you liked it," I muttered, picturing how they'd look strung up by their toes.

"Liked it?" Tommy chortled. "We loved it! It couldn't have gone better if we'd planned it ourselves!"

Josh joined him with a hearty laugh. "At least you picked a good day for it," he pointed out. "Everybody else is sweltering. You're the only one who figured out how to beat the heat by taking a swim in the ring."

Tommy reached out and plucked at the pocket of my breeches, pulling it open so that he could look inside. "Here, fishy, fishy," he cooed.

"Oh, for Pete's sake!" I snapped, pulling away. "Would you two grow up!"

"Us?" Josh asked.

"Yes, you," I said, laughing in spite of myself.

The trouble was that even though the joke was on me, I had to admit the whole thing really was kind of funny. I mean, lots of riders fall off their horses, but how many manage to do it right in the middle of a fish pond?

"Alexandra!"

"Whoops," I said under my breath. I'd recognize that bellow anywhere.

"I think that's our cue to get lost," Tommy said and ducked out of sight into the tack room.

"Want me to hang around for moral support?" Josh offered, surprising me for the second time that day. Then it occurred to me that probably all he really wanted to do was stay around long enough to make sure that I didn't implicate Tommy and him as accessories to the crime.

"No, you go on," I said, trying to sound a whole lot braver than I felt. "I'll be along in a minute."

Jack was standing in the middle of the aisle that ran between the rows of stalls.

"Alexandra Anderson, just what exactly did you think you were doing out there in the ring?" The way that loud voice of his boomed up and down the aisle drew just about everybody's attention. Even those who were working stopped what they were doing and turned around to stare.

I sidled closer, hoping to bring the volume down a notch. It was bad enough being yelled at. I didn't want the entire world to listen, "Riding the course?"

"I could see that!" Jack shouted. "What I want to know is, why?"

Now how on earth was I going to answer that? If I told him the truth, Tommy and Josh would be in every bit as much trouble as I. Not that they didn't deserve it.

"I wanted to see if I could do it," I said finally.

"Well I guess you had that question answered for you." Jack's tone was somewhat softer. When I looked up, I could have sworn that the beginning of a smile was twitching around the corners of his mouth. Then he grew stern once more. "You do realize what a foolish chance you took, riding that horse over a course he wasn't the least bit ready for?"

Trust Jack to worry about the horse's welfare first and the people second, I thought. "Yes, Jack."

"You got off lucky this time. I had a look at the gelding when Pete brought him in a minute ago and he didn't look any the worse for wear." He let that sink in for a minute before adding, "Which is more than I can say for you."

"Yes, I know."

"Do you have any dry clothes in the tack room?"

I nodded.

"Then get in there and change. And get some trees in those boots, or they'll be ruined."

"Yes, sir." Figuring I'd been dismissed, I turned to leave.

"Oh, and Alex? I trust you learned something from this?"

So help me, I couldn't resist a smile. "I sure did. Never drop a horse, even one you trust, one stride in front of a water jump."

Jack's laughter rang out up and down the length of the aisle. "A good thing to know. See that you remember it."

"Yes, sir."

All things considered, I thought as I turned toward the tack room once more, I'd gotten off a good bit lighter than I'd expected.

Pete, Tommy, and Josh were waiting for me inside.

"Whew," said Pete. "Did you ever get lucky! I thought he was really going to read you the riot act! Instead all he did was ask you a few questions, then tell you to change your clothes."

"I know what you mean," said Tommy. "I've seen him kick riders out of the barn for lesser infractions than that."

"Thanks a lot for telling me now," I told him sarcastically.

"Don't thank me," Tommy replied. "You're the one who braved the dragon and lived to tell about it. I wonder what's up."

Josh, sitting in the corner of the room on a bale of hay, spoke up for the first time. "Have you ever heard of something called the riders' revolt?"

The three of us looked blankly at each other.

"It happened at the Devon Horse Show just about twenty years ago."

Josh had our full attention. He'd been riding with Jack longer than anyone else we knew, and had lots of anecdotes that had happened back when Jack himself was one of the leading competitors on the circuit.

"The whole thing started when the American Horse Show Association changed some of its rules without notifying any of the exhibitors. Devon was the first show to come along after the new rules went into effect, and all at once riders were finding themselves excused from the classes for committing infractions that they knew nothing about. Understandably, they got pretty mad.

"The show officials said that rules were rules, and refused to talk things over. At that point the top exhibitors, figuring that they had no other choice, revolted."

"What do you mean, they revolted?" I asked. "What did they do?"

"Apparently one of the new rules was some sort of dress code. In protest, the riders dressed up in the most outrageous costumes they could find, wearing war paint, and silly hats, and flapping T-shirts. They rode their horses into the ring bareback, or double, and jumped the courses backward.

"The ringmaster went crazy but there was nothing he could do to stop them. Finally the show management was forced to halt the show and sit down and discuss their demands. Eventually the new rules were dropped, and everything went back to the way it had been."

"Is there any relevance to this story?" asked Tommy. "Or do you just like having the floor?"

"Of course there is." Josh smiled, his dimple deepening once more. "Jack himself would never admit it, but the way I heard things, he was one of the leaders of the protest. Even though he knew it might lead to his getting suspended from showing, he still went ahead and did it anyway.''

Josh paused to glance in my direction. ''That,'' he said meaningfully, ''is why he didn't take you apart the way you probably deserved.''

''I still don't get it,'' Pete said with a frown.

I was glad he spoke up because I didn't get it either.

''It's a matter of guts, Ali. You've got them or you never would have tackled that course in the first place. Jack may not approve of what you did, but I'll bet anything he respects the fact that you were brave enough to try.''

''Either that, or stupid enough,'' I offered.

''Same difference,'' Tommy said with a shrug. ''Any way you look at it, you still proved our point.''

''I did not!'' I cried in outrage. ''Dare Me jumped every fence out there but one. And it wasn't the highest, or the widest. All he needed was a little practice with water and he'd have handled that one too.''

Tommy started to laugh although I couldn't for the life of me see what was so funny. ''Should we tell her?'' he asked Josh as I looked back and forth between them.

"I suppose," Josh said slowly. I wondered what he had done to make him look so sheepish. "To tell the truth," he admitted, "we were never worried for a minute about Dare Me making it around the course."

"But . . ." I sputtered.

"It was you!" Tommy chortled. "Josh and I had a bet about whether or not *you* could do it. Thanks a lot, Alex," he said, clapping me on the shoulder. "You've just bought me a dinner at the best steak house in town."

Hearing that made me so mad that I could have gladly strangled both of them. Instead, with as much dignity as I could muster in wet breeches and boots that squished with every step, I spun around and left the room. My face reddened as the sound of their laughter followed me out of the barn.

Chapter Two

Mornings have always been my favorite time of day. I'm one of those people who wake up really wide awake and alert, as soon as the sun rises. In the winter, I usually snuggle back under the covers for a while with a good book. But in the summer, I can't wait to be up and doing.

Bitsy Thornton, who is my best friend and my roommate when we're on the circuit, is just the opposite. She thinks that nothing good can ever come of a day that has to start before noon. Heaven help us both on the mornings when she has an early class, and I have to make sure that she's up and over at the showgrounds on time.

Bitsy comes from way down south, Georgia to be exact. Just as you'd expect, she has that slow, drawly way of talking that sounds like honey melting on a warm day. I've seen it in action and it has the guaranteed effect of making any boy within earshot fall all over himself to be of service. Add to that the most gorgeous, long, blond hair, ivory skin and big green eyes, and you can see how she has all the makings of your basic femme fatale.

The funny thing about Bitsy, though, is that she doesn't seem to realize that. Beneath an exterior that most girls would die for, she has the same insecurities as everybody else I know. She thinks her nose is too big, and she's always on one diet or another, although I, for one, can't see much of anything wrong with her figure at all.

If she's dissatisfied with what she has, I shudder to think what she'd do if she had my figure to contend with. Not that things are hopeless by any means, but everywhere she seems to think she's got too much of a good thing, nature has endowed me with too little. Pete, who shares my coloring— auburn hair, blue eyes and freckles—says it's a good thing I wear my hair long, otherwise no one would be able to tell us apart.

Bitsy is the baby of her family, which means that she doesn't have to deal with things like obnoxious younger brothers. It also means that when she was little, she learned to sleep through everything short of a nuclear explosion. The next morning, when I tried to get her up so that we could go over to the show grounds early, was a perfect example.

First I pulled aside the heavy motel curtains to let some light into the room. A shaft of sunlight fell across the bed and onto her face. With a muffled groan she turned over and buried her head under the covers.

"Rise and shine," I said cheerfully. I was anxious to get over to the hunt club so that I could take Dare Me out while it was still cool.

"Mmmph," she mumbled, burrowing down even deeper under the blankets. "What time is it?"

"Come on," I said, purposely ignoring her question. I peeled back one edge of the sheet and looked underneath. "It's a beautiful day...."

"What time is it?"

"It's bright and sunny—"

"What time is it?" Sleepily Bitsy sat up and yawned. In her flower-sprigged nightgown, she looked about six years old.

"Seven o'clock," I said quickly. "But—"

"Seven o'clock!" Bitsy shrieked. She flopped back down onto the bed and pulled the covers up over her head once more. "Get out of my bed, you Yankee! I swear," she mumbled from beneath the blanket, "you Northerners are so pushy!"

"And you Southerners are soft and lazy," I retorted with a grin. It was a long-standing joke between us.

"Go away!" The lump under the blanket shook its fist menacingly. "Wake me up when morning really comes, and not before!"

"But I want to get over to the show grounds early so that I can work Dare Me on the course before everybody else shows up to school."

"Go ahead," Bitsy said. "I'll catch a ride with somebody later."

"Okay. You do know that your first class is at ten?"

"Mmm-hmm."

"You won't go back to sleep and miss it?"

"Uhn-uhn."

Since there really wasn't much else I could do, I gathered up my gear and left. I did, however, stop at the front desk on my way out where I left a wake-up call for nine o'clock. At least she wouldn't be able to sleep the whole morning away.

Just my luck, the first person I ran into when I reached the hunt club was Josh Connelly. Even though it was June, the early morning air was still quite cool. Like me, he was wearing a cotton sweater over his shirt, and had zipped on a worn pair of leather chaps to protect his buff-colored breeches so that they would still be clean for his classes later.

"You're up early," he said. He fell into step beside me as I stopped at the cafeteria tent to pick up a cup of hot coffee.

"So are you."

The counter woman handed us two steaming, Styrofoam cups. We paid for them, then stopped at the end of the table to add milk and sugar.

"I'm always up this time of day," said Josh. "I love early mornings. When I sleep in, I feel as though I've wasted half the day."

"I know what you mean," I agreed. Of one accord, we left the tent and headed over to the stabling area. "Bitsy likes nothing more than to stay in bed all day. It drives me crazy sometimes."

Sipping his coffee, Josh only nodded in agreement, and we walked the rest of the way in a companionable silence.

It was funny, I thought, that even with him there beside me, I still felt free to enjoy the morning sights and sounds. Usually when I'm with a boy, I'm trying so hard to make a good impression that I'm not aware of anything but him. I'm either chattering on about his favorite subjects, or else listening attentively while he does.

Yet with Josh, I didn't feel obliged to fill up every minute with talk. Probably because I wasn't trying to make a good impression. Who cared what Josh Connelly thought anyway?

Though it was early, the barns were already a hub of activity. Horses that were going to be shown in the hunter classes later that day were standing in the cross-ties having their manes and tails braided. Those that needed exercise were being lunged in wide circles out in the field. A long line had already formed near the concrete drain where the horses stood to have their baths.

Pete, who knew my habits, had made sure that Dare Me was among the first to be fed, so that by the time I arrived, he was ready to be ridden. Picking up my saddle and bridle in the tack room, I lugged them down the aisle to his stall.

"Taking him out for a hack?" Jack asked, sticking in his head over the webbing stall guard that served as a door.

I nodded as I slipped the bit into Dare Me's mouth.

"Don't do too much," Jack advised. "Especially after yesterday, he doesn't need it."

I absorbed the subtle dig in silence.

"Good old guy," Jack murmured. He reached in to scratch between the gelding's ears. As I settled the flat saddle on his back, Dare Me stepped closer to the doorway, offering himself shamelessly to be made a fuss over.

"He isn't getting any younger," Jack murmured. Then, louder, in my direction, he added, "How old is he anyway?"

"Fifteen last January." I stooped down to draw the girth up around his belly.

Though fifteen wasn't ancient by horse standards, it was certainly well into middle age. I was Dare Me's third owner, my parents having bought him for me on my twelfth birthday when he was already eleven years old. Counting back now, I realized that he'd probably already been a regular on the circuit by the time I entered grade school.

"You'd never know it to ride him, though," I said. "I swear, sometimes he acts just like a two-year-old."

"Don't we all." Jack sent a meaningful glance in my direction.

I flashed him a winning smile. "I thought you'd forgiven me."

"Accepted, yes. Forgiveness takes longer. Pull one more stunt like that and you're out of here. You know that, don't you?"

"Yes, Jack."

He opened the door so that I could lead Dare Me out into the aisle. "Good, just so we understand each other. Now get that horse out of here and give him a nice, quiet hack—the kind he should have had yesterday before you started getting crazy ideas.''

Dare Me and I spent a pleasant hour on the maze of bridle paths surrounding the hunt club. We walked and trotted down the cool, sunlit trails, popping over fallen trees that formed low jumps across the path, and stopping occasionally to admire a pheasant or a deer. By the time we got back and I had him cooled out and rubbed down, the show was already in full swing.

Stopping at the horse show office, I placed a call to Bitsy. There was no answer in the room, so I assumed she must be on her way. Though the junior hunter classes weren't due to start until mid-afternoon, Bitsy was showing a large pony as well, and that class started in less than an hour.

The pony's owner was a child who had lost interest in riding, so his parents were looking to sell. They figured, with good reason as I saw it, that a few good wins on the circuit would up the asking price. Bitsy, who at five foot three was small enough to still look good on a pony, had taken the mount as a catch-ride the week before.

When I returned to the stabling area after making the call, Bitsy was already there. Even though it was almost ten o'clock, I could tell from the fuzzy, sort of blank expression on her face that she had just gotten out of bed. Then again, Bitsy is the only person I know who actually looks good when she first wakes up in the morning.

Now she was sitting on one of the big tack trunks in the aisle, talking to Tommy who was getting ready to show Lobo in the junior jumper class. Ever since I've known her, she's always had sort of a thing about Tommy. I've never been able to understand it at all, especially since she's usually such a reasonable person in other ways. I guess there's just no accounting for some people's taste in boys.

The funny thing is that either Tommy is too dumb to realize that she's interested or, for some reason, he's decided to play hard to get. Believe me, if I had as little going for me as he does, I'd be thrilled if *anyone* liked me, much less a girl who's as great as Bitsy.

"Tell me about the course," she was saying. I could tell from the way she fastened those big green eyes of hers on him that she wasn't the slightest bit interested in the course.

"Why don't you ask Alex?" Tommy replied, with a low chuckle that really grated on my nerves. "She rode it yesterday."

"Okay," Bitsy turned to me with a mock serious expression on her face. "Other than that, Mrs. Lincoln, how was the play?"

Trust Bitsy with that Southern charm of hers to play the role of the diplomat.

"It was easy," I said. "A real cinch. Even a baby could do it. And," I added, leveling a glare at Tommy, "probably will."

"Aaargh!" Tommy cried, clutching his hands to his heart as though pulling out the blade of a dagger. "I've been wounded to the core!"

"Not again," said Jack, who was passing by. "Tommy, don't you have a class to ride? I'll be up in the schooling area in two minutes, and I'll expect to see you there."

"Yes, sir!" Tommy picked up his hard hat, jammed it down on top of his head, tied his number around his waist and hurried down to the cross tie at the end of the aisle where Lobo was waiting.

"What about you?" I said to Bitsy. I saw by my watch that it was already a few minutes after ten. "Hasn't your class already started?"

"I checked on the way in and the pony class before mine was running late. Besides, Glory's number is way at the end of the jumping order. They won't be calling for me for at least an hour." Stifling a yawn, she picked herself up off the trunk. "I suppose I may as well head on out, though. Do you want to come?"

"Sure." We left the tent together.

It's a good thing she and I were such good friends. Otherwise I really could have resented how easily things seemed to fall into her lap. And she simply took all the marvelous good fortune she had for granted.

Take horses, for instance. I was one of those little girls who was certifiably horse crazy. My parents are pretty athletic, as these things go, but they never cared a fig about horses. Being the reasonable sort, however, they decided to humor me. They were certain, I'm sure, that if they let me go through my phase, I'd probably outgrow it.

They never loved the shows the way I did. Nor did they appreciate the amount of time the shows took, especially during the school year when they'd have preferred that I study.

Bitsy, on the other hand, simply grew up with all of this handed to her. She was one of those children who actually rode before she could walk, since her mother used to balance her up on the front of her own saddle before Bitsy was even a year old.

Both her parents are very much involved with horses. Her father is what Bitsy calls a gentleman farmer, which, I gather from other things she's said, means that he has a plantation roughly the size of Rhode Island. He breeds horses, and the whole family loves to ride and hunt. To top it off, she has two brothers who ride steeplechase in Virginia and Maryland.

When it came time for Bitsy to have her own horse, all she had to do was walk out the back door and pick one. And it wasn't a case of her parents allowing her to go on the circuit, as it was with mine. Instead, they encouraged her all the way.

Besides that, Bitsy is what you might call a natural rider. She has a great seat, and the softest hands I've ever seen. All she has to do is climb up on a horse and automatically she looks good. Not like me, always worrying about whether my back is straight or my heels are down.

The only problem with all this good fortune she has, is that Bitsy really doesn't seem to care about it one way or another. She fell into riding because it was expected of her, without ever stopping to think about whether or not that was really what she wanted to do. I glanced sideways at her. Yes, as usual, she was taking it all very calmly. In fact, she didn't even look fully awake yet.

We stopped by the Sunnyledge Farm setup to pick up Glory Be, the mare she was supposed to ride. Then we headed on up to the outside course at the end of the polo field where the ponies were being shown. I watched her warm up the mare, then set up a few practice jumps for her in the schooling ring.

When her number was called, Bitsy put in her usual smooth trip, which was just the sort of thing that the pony judges were looking for. Nobody was surprised twenty minutes later when she and Glory won the class. We handed the pony, still wearing the fluttering blue ribbon pinned to her bridle, back to one of the Sunnyledge grooms, then headed over to the main ring to watch the jumpers.

As we settled into the grandstand with our cans of diet soda, Tommy and Lobo were just riding out onto the course.

"Go, Tommy!" Bitsy stood up and screamed.

"Geez," I said when she sat back down in her seat, her face flushed with a happy smile. "Did you have to make all that noise?"

"I just wanted him to know that we were rooting for him."

"You," I corrected, "are the one rooting for him, not me. Besides, I'm sure he already knows that. You always root for Tommy."

"I do, don't I?"

"Yes, you do. And that's more than you can say for him. Has he ever come over to the outside course to watch you show Blithe Spirit in junior hunters?"

"Now that you mention it," she said slowly, "no."

"I didn't think so," I added. "It isn't just Tommy, you know. Most boys are like that. When they do something that's halfway decent, they expect everyone to fall all over them. Then when we do something absolutely fantastic, we're lucky if they even notice at all."

"I know the boys down home sure act that way," Bitsy agreed, "but I was hoping that, up here, things might be different." She sighed. "I guess it's true what my mama says, 'You can always tell a rooster by his strut.'"

Bitsy is always passing along these sayings that her mama told her. Unfortunately, a good deal of the time, I can't figure out what they're supposed to mean at all. This time, however, it made perfect sense.

Looking out over the course, I saw Josh on China Doll just entering the ring. Together, Bitsy and I watched as he guided the mare deftly around the tricky course. Since it was the second day, the jumps were now even more difficult than those Dare Me and I had faced yesterday. No matter what else I had to say about Josh, I had to admit one thing. That boy could really ride.

Of the original thirty competing in the class, eight including both Josh and Tommy were called back for a jump-off against the clock. In the event that the horses went clean once more, the one with the shortest time would win.

Tommy, as usual, was flashy and spectacular. Lobo raced around the course at a frenetic pace like a wind-up toy gone mad. The gallery oohed and aahed with each obstacle he cleared. By the time he jumped the last fence for a clean round and the best time so far, the crowd was on its feet cheering.

Three other horses went clean, but none was able to match Lobo's time. Last to enter the ring was Josh on China Doll. Talk about pressure! In his place, I'd have been quaking in my boots, but Josh looked as calm and collected as if he was merely out for a quiet hack in the country.

As opposed to Tommy, who'd ridden the course with daring and verve, Josh's style was pure poetry. There were none of those flamboyant moves that hooked the audience, but no wasted motion either. Whereas Tommy had gone for speed, Josh settled for finding the shortest distance between two points. He cut every corner that could be cut, and then some. China Doll, who was supple and agile and light on her feet, managed to jump out of pockets that a lesser horse would have found impossible.

When they raced past the clock at the end of the course, and the winning time flashed up on the board, I found myself up on my feet, cheering wildly, "Way to go, Josh!"

Setting down her soda can, Bitsy regarded me mildly. "And you said *I* made a spectacle out of myself."

"You did," I agreed as we climbed down from the stands. "And now so have I, so we're even. I guess we'll just have to go on rooming together. After all, who else would have us?"

Bitsy smiled. "You know, Alex, as Yankees go, you're not half bad."

That's one of the things I like about Bitsy. She really knows how to give a compliment.

Chapter Three

By the time the weekend rolled around, Bitsy and I were feeling pretty pleased with ourselves. She and Blithe Spirit had racked up eight points toward the championship in the large junior hunters. Dare Me and I, competing in the small division, had won the hack and a class over fences for a total of ten.

In fact, pleased wasn't really the half of it. Smug was more like it. Especially since, after their early triumphs, Josh and Tommy had both faded rather badly. Probably due to too much partying, I decided, watching Tommy drag himself, bleary-eyed, into the tack room on Saturday morning.

"Late night, last night?" I asked, winking at Bitsy behind Tommy's back.

He groaned some sort of reply, then flopped down heavily into one of the blue director's chairs.

"Would you like a cup of coffee?" Bitsy asked sympathetically. I could just see her maternal instincts sprouting all over the place.

Tommy muttered something unintelligible. Bitsy hurried off to do his bidding.

"Well, now that you've got her running around at your beck and call, I hope you're planning to rouse yourself enough to say thank you when she returns," I said nastily.

"Mmmphh," Tommy grumbled with his eyes closed.

"Articulate as always, are you?"

Tommy opened one eye. To my surprise, he began to smile. The way he looked, it's a wonder the effort didn't kill him. "Articulate," he said. "A-r-t-i-c-u-l-a-t-e. Capable of speaking clearly, as in, 'The governor's speech to the state assembly was highly articulate.'"

"Very good."

"Yes," Tommy agreed. "It was, wasn't it?"

"Is there any particular reason why you're acting as though you've just signed up for the state spelling bee, or is this just a new fad I haven't caught up on yet?"

"Fad," Tommy repeated, his eyes alight with a mischievous gleam. "F-a-d—"

"Oh for Pete's sake!" I snapped, wishing that Bitsy would hurry up and get back from her mission of mercy. She and I were planning to go out and have a look at the course the jump crew was setting up in the main ring for the day's equitation classes.

"Don't you like my new vocabulary?"

"Sure," I replied. "It beats those noises you used to try and pass off as conversation in the past. But why all the bother now?"

"Third year English Lit. If I don't pass the course, my parents will kill me. I may as well kiss college goodbye. I have a paper due Monday. I was up all night last night, trying to get it finished so I could put it in the early mail this morning."

"You stayed up all last night *studying*?" For some reason the idea struck me as absurdly funny. For all their macho strutting and posturing, it looked as though Tommy and Josh's night life wasn't any wilder than ours.

"What's the matter with that?" Tommy glared at me.

"Nothing," I said quickly. "I just didn't expect it, that's all. I mean, it *is* summer. All my classes ended weeks ago."

"So did mine. That's just the problem. You know how the circuit is..."

Tommy didn't finish the thought, but I understood. I *did* know how the circuit was. It ran from early February in Florida to late November in Toronto, making not the slightest concession for kids who were supposed to be in school.

Some got around the problem by traveling with tutors. Others handled their courses by mail. Still others went to school three days a week, then flew off to the shows on Thursday mornings. Whatever route you chose, it wasn't easy.

My parents had always insisted that I confine the bulk of my showing to summer vacations. Since I had my sights zeroed in on a good college education, I could hardly disagree. Knowing however, that both Josh and Tommy had been on the road since February, it was easy to understand how he'd managed to get himself in trouble.

"There just never seemed to be enough time to get the assignments done and handed in," Tommy explained. "The few I did manage to complete didn't get very good grades. Finally the teacher gave me an incomplete, and told me I was taking English Lit as a makeup course this summer. It's my last chance, as far as that goes. If I don't pass it this time I'm dead."

"So that's why you've been boning up on your vocabulary?"

"Josh said his teachers are always impressed by lots of big words. It makes them think you're smarter than you really are.

"He's been tutoring me some," Tommy continued. "Apparently the school he goes to is really progressive. Even though we're in the same grade, he already did all the stuff I'm doing now, last year. He's a whole lot smarter than you'd think, just looking at him. Did you know he's already been to Princeton for his college interview, and he's planning on applying there for early decision in the fall?"

"Josh?" I repeated incredulously. "Josh Connelly?"

"Sure," said Tommy, giving me a weird look. "Who else?"

Bitsy finally returned, carrying Tommy's steaming coffee in a white Styrofoam cup. "Here, drink this," she said in her soft Southern drawl. "I was going to add cream and sugar, but then I decided that from the looks of you, you needed all the kick you could get."

"Thanks a lot." Tommy sipped at the hot, black brew cautiously. "It's not my fault I had lots to do last night."

"Oh no?" Bitsy's brow rose.

"He and Josh were studying," I interjected, to put her out of her misery. "Tommy's taking a makeup course in English Lit."

"Hey, do you mind?" Tommy glared at me across the tack room. "It's not as if the whole world has to know!"

"Well excu-u-u-se me," I said, surprised by his reaction. After all, it wasn't as though I'd made the announcement over the loudspeakers or anything.

"English Lit?" Bitsy smiled. "That's always been one of my best subjects. Which authors are you studying?"

"One of *your* best subjects?" Tommy hooted. "That's a laugh. Why, you can't even speak the language right!"

"Oh yeah?" I retorted, leaping to her defense. "You're a fine one to talk, Mr. Articulate. At least we know better than to run off at the mouth when we haven't got even the slightest idea what we're talking about!"

As comebacks went, it wasn't great, but it was the best I could do on short notice. "Come on," I said to Bitsy, "Let's go see what kind of shape the course is in."

When we arrived at the ring, we saw that the fences had already been put up and everything was ready for the start of the first class. All week long, we had been riding in different divisions. Today, for the first time, we would be competing against each other.

There were three equitation classes, and all were important in determining the best junior riders in the country. Two, the Medal and the Maclay, had finals in November. In order to qualify, each of us had to win three blue ribbons in each of the two classes before the middle of October.

Both Josh and Tommy, who had been on the circuit since February, already had two of the wins they each needed. I had had the good fortune to pick up my first at the Devon Show two weeks earlier. Bitsy, who was just starting out, needed everything.

"Tough course," she commented, measuring the height and width of the fences with a practiced eye. She gestured toward a sharply angled corner at the near end of the field. "That turn's going to be trouble."

"Blithe can handle it. Don't worry, we'll show those two clowns who knows how to ride around here."

Bitsy was unusually quiet as we turned back to collect our mounts. I knew if I waited long enough she'd blurt out what was on her mind. Finally she did.

"You don't really think I talk funny, do you?"

The question was so ludicrous that I almost laughed. Then I saw the expression on her face. "Of course not," I declared. "I think the way you speak is beautiful. It's all soft and slow—"

"That's exactly the problem," Bitsy broke in. "It takes me so long to say anything, that people are probably bored by the time I get the words out."

"No they're not. Not even Tommy, and he has the attention span of a gnat. You shouldn't let him get to you. The only reason he said those things was because he was feeling mean and ornery after having to stay up all last night.

"Just you wait," I added. "As soon as he's had some sleep he'll be back to apologize, you'll see."

Back at the barn, Jack was overseeing two grooms as they put the finishing touches on the equitation horses.

"You girls ready?" he asked.

"Yes, Jack," we replied in unison, then looked at each other and smiled. It was like being back in second grade.

"You've been up to see the course and check out the jumping order?"

Again we answered in the affirmative.

"Then what are you doing wasting time down here?" he yelled. "Get on these animals and get them warmed up! Your class starts in ten minutes. I'll see you in half that in the schooling ring!"

"You know," Bitsy whispered out of the side of her mouth as we unhooked the two horses from the cross ties and led them down the aisle. "If his bite is worse than his bark, I don't even want to know about it!"

The U.S. Equestrian Team class came first. I really managed to blow it. The turn Bitsy had pointed out was going to be trouble. She handled it just fine. I was the one who swung too wide and missed the line on the fence. Not surprisingly, I was left out of the ribbons as was Tommy who rode the course as though he was half asleep, which he probably was.

Josh, who looked marginally better than Tommy did after their all-nighter, pulled in a fourth to Bitsy's third.

"You guys better sharpen up!" Jack growled at us irritably. He was waiting at the gate as we left the ring after the class. "Any more sloppy performances like that and you're liable to find yourselves home watching the finals at Madison Square Garden on cable TV!"

"Yes, Jack," we chorused.

The thing about Jack is that he's a perfectionist. He absolutely cannot bear it when one of his kids lets him down. If he decides you're giving less than one hundred percent effort, he really comes down hard. Only no matter how good you are, nobody wins all the time. Sometimes I wished that Jack realized that.

"Whew!" said Josh, when we arrived back in the tack room. He took off his jacket and flung it over the back of a chair. "I guess we deserved that."

"Speak for yourself." Bitsy buffed her fingernails against the front of her shirt. "I thought I rode rather well. I can't help it if you Yankees are having an off day."

"Listen to her!" Tommy cried. He took off his number and raised it above his head like a flag. "The South shall rise again!"

Josh frowned at him with mock sternness. "It would probably succeed too, if we had to rely on you for our defense. All I can say is that if you keep riding like that, there'll be one less person I have to beat when I get to New York."

"Oh yeah?" I cried. "Who even says you're going to New York? You haven't qualified yet, you know."

"It's still early. We've got four more months."

"The rate you're going, you'll probably need them."

"You're a fine one to talk," said Tommy. "At least, we've each got two of our blues, which is more than either one of you can say."

"That's because you've been working on it since February," Bitsy pointed out. She was usually too much of a lady to get drawn into our spats, so I figured she must still be mad at Tommy for the things he'd said to her earlier. "If we'd been around that long, we'd probably have qualified by now."

"Sure," said Josh. "Tell me another one."

"We would!" I maintained, not because I necessarily thought it was true, but because Tommy and Josh were being so obnoxious. Besides, Bitsy was my friend, and I'd stick up for her no matter what.

"Well if you two are feeling so sure of yourselves," said Josh, "how about putting your money where your mouths are?"

"Any time!" I wondered what he was up to now. The last time he'd gotten that sort of gleam in his eye, I'd ended up in the bottom of a fish pond in the main ring.

"Right now suits me just fine," said Josh. "How about a little bet? Girls against the guys. Whichever pair is first to qualify for New York and Harrisburg wins."

"Sounds good to me," I cried.

"Well it sounds terrible to me," Bitsy put in. She drew me aside. "Has it occurred to you that they've got an unfair advantage? They already have four wins between them, while we only have one."

"What's the matter?" asked Tommy. "Can't take the competition?"

"Of course we can!" Bitsy retorted. "After all, everybody knows girls are much better riders than boys are."

"Oh really?" said Josh. "Just who is everybody?"

"Look at the evidence," I said, leaping in. "More of the high-score awards are won by girls than boys."

"That's because there are more girls riding."

"And riding better, too!"

"Okay," Josh laughed, looking at Tommy. "I can see we're just going to have to prove this to them." Then he turned back to Bitsy and me. "Unless you don't feel you're up to the challenge?"

"Phooey!" Bitsy cried. "We'll be glad to take you on. And we'll win too!"

"Speaking of winning," I asked, "just what exactly are the stakes here?"

"Let me see." Josh paused. He looked at me and grinned. "Everybody knows how much you like to eat, Ali. How about if the losers take the winners out to a victory dinner after the Garden, in New York?"

"Good idea," Bitsy agreed. "I hope you guys remember to bring lots of money."

"You were sounding pretty sure of yourself back there," I said several minutes later as we walked over to the cafeteria tent to get ourselves some lunch.

"I was, wasn't I?" she said. "I just hope we don't end up getting creamed.

Stepping up to the counter, we ordered our food, a hamburger with the works for me, and a salad for Bitsy who was, as always, watching her weight. "Why should we? I meant what I said back there— girls really are better riders. Besides, if Tommy keeps staying up till all hours studying, he'll be lucky to qualify at all, much less first."

We paid for our food, carried it over to an empty table and sat down. Bitsy eyed my hamburger wistfully, then dribbled some vinegar onto her bowl of lettuce and dug in. "Is that really what he was doing last night, studying?"

"That's what he told me. He said that he'd had to take an incomplete in one of his courses this year, and that Josh, of all people, was coaching him so that he'd pass the makeup course."

"I don't know why you say that," said Bitsy. "I happen to know for a fact that Josh is very smart. Just because you two don't always get along doesn't mean he hasn't got a brain."

"It has nothing to do with how we get along. It's just that his ego is so large, I always just assumed there was no room left in there for anything else."

"In case you haven't noticed, there are plenty of other girls around here who are interested in Josh Connelly, even if you aren't."

"Oh really?"

"Yes, really," Bitsy said. "Although if you'd stop putting him off the way you do, I'm sure you wouldn't have any problem jumping to the head of the line."

"Me put him off?" That's a habit of mine. Whenever anyone accuses me of doing something that I know I do, but don't want to admit to, I pretend I haven't the slightest idea what they're talking about.

After three years of rooming together, however, Bitsy knew me entirely too well. "I swear," she said with a dramatic sigh that played beautifully with her soft Southern drawl. "The way you Yankees go on, it's a wonder you ever won the war at all."

"At least now you're admitting we won," I said pleased to see the subject changed. "It seems, I remember, you once tried to convince me that the outcome was still a matter of opinion."

"Down home where I come from, it still is. See what's happened to me, spendin' all this time up here the last few years? I'm even beginning to think like you."

Tilting her head back, Bitsy finished off the last of her diet soda, then lobbed the empty can into the garbage.

"We'd better get a move on before you-know-who realizes we're late and comes after us."

The rest of the afternoon couldn't have gone more perfectly if I'd planned it myself. First Bitsy rode her mare Blithe Spirit to a first-place finish in the Medal. Then Dare Me and I finally got our act together, and managed to win the Maclay.

At this rate, I decided smugly, as the ringmaster pinned the blue ribbon to Dare Me's bridle, we'd have that bet won in no time. The fact that Josh was behind me in second place made the victory all the sweeter.

"Close," I said, taunting him as we left the ring, "but no cigar."

Josh grinned. For the life of me, I couldn't see what he had to be so pleased about. "You know, Ali," he said, looking me up and down, "you're getting better."

"What do you mean *getting* better?" No way was I going to admit that he was getting to me. "I've always been a better rider than you."

"Not your riding," said Josh, his grin still firmly in place. "Just you."

I was too astonished to say a word. I just watched Josh move away with that jaunty, swinging stride of his. He'd gone a good five yards before I even remembered to close my mouth.

Chapter Four

On the horse show circuit, Mondays are travel days. They constitute a sort of limbo period between the show that ends on Sunday and the next one that begins, after a day devoted to practice, the following Wednesday. Monday is the day spent packing up and moving on.

That Monday, the drive was a short one, from the Ox Ridge Hunt Club in Darien, to the Fairfield Hunt Club in Westport, less than twenty miles away. Once there, the routine was the same as always. The grooms got the horses bedded down, then went to work setting up the tack room and making sure everything was in order for the start of the show.

As usual, Bitsy and I went straight to the motel. Since Jack's secretary knows everybody's schedule months in advance, she simply picks the most convenient place and reserves a block of rooms. That way, all his riders stay together, and everybody knows where everybody else is. As almost his entire stable is made up of junior riders, it's a plan the parents approve of heartily.

"I guess we showed them but good," Bitsy said as we tossed our suitcases up on the bed and began to unpack.

"That's for sure. Just think, after only three weeks, you and I have accomplished almost as much as Tommy and Josh have in the past four months. At this rate, we'll have them beaten in no time!"

"It would be no more than they deserve." She paused to lift out a delicate blue silk blouse. "Boys." She sighed. "Why do they have to be so hard to figure out?"

She was talking about Tommy of course. As far as I was concerned, it would take a team of scientists to figure out what was going on inside that thick skull of his.

"Maybe you ought to try something different," I suggested. "It might be that he takes you for granted because you're so available. Maybe you should try ignoring him for a week or two, play a little harder to get."

Bitsy flopped down on the bed. "I'm just not the type to play games like that. I never have been. And despite the fact that my mama told me most Yankees are a sneaky, conniving lot, neither are you, Alexandra Anderson. Shame on you for even suggesting it!"

"I was only trying to help." I sat down beside her. "Speaking of your mama, she seems to have a saying for just about everything. What sort of advice did she give you about trying to get a man?"

"*My mama?* Why she'd be horrified by the very idea of going after a man at all!"

"Do tell," I drawled.

"My mama's a lady, through and through. Down home, it's the man who comes courtin', not the other way around. A lady receives him on the veranda with cool tea, warm biscuits and fresh flowers. If he's lucky and behaves himself very nicely, he gets invited back again."

I swallowed a laugh as I tried to picture my very efficient, very modern mom sitting on a veranda and sipping iced tea as she received male callers.

"I know," Bitsy said, misinterpreting my laugh. "It didn't do me much good, either."

"That's not what struck me so funny," I said quickly. "It's just that I was thinking our mothers didn't have very much in common, that's all."

"Why? What did yours tell you?"

"Nothing about flowers and biscuits, that's for sure!" I collapsed back onto the pillows as we both giggled together.

"To tell the truth," I admitted finally, "my mom wasn't a whole lot more help on the subject than yours. All she ever said was that the most important thing was to go out with a boy you knew you could be friends with—that good looks were fine, but they didn't mean a thing if you didn't have anything to talk about."

"There, you see?" said Bitsy, her expression brightening. "Tommy and I should be great for each other. At least we have plenty to talk about."

"The only problem with that is he's always the one doing all the talking, and you're always the one doing all the listening."

"That's my mama's influence again. Didn't yours ever tell you it pays to be a good listener?"

"My mom's a firm believer in speaking up. She drives my dad crazy sometimes. No matter what's on her mind, she just blurts it right out."

"So that's where you get it from. And here I just thought that was general Yankee rudeness."

"Hah!" I picked up a pillow and swatted her over the head with it. "I'll show you Yankee rudeness!"

The problem with tackling Bitsy is that I knew from experience she always gave as good as she got. Those fragile looks of hers were deceptive, matched as they were with a tough, wiry sort of strength and a stubborn streak nearly as wide as my own.

By the time I declared myself the victor ten minutes later, the room was a shambles and we were both breathing hard. Bitsy, who had tangled her feet in the bedspread as she launched an attack, was lying on the floor. Without conceding defeat, she hauled herself up, grabbed her toiletries case off the dresser and headed for the shower. Just like that I was left in the outer room all by myself to clean up the mess.

So much for the thrill of victory, I thought, glaring at the closed bathroom door.

No sooner had I started to pick up the pillows and toss them back on the bed than there was a loud knock at the door. I crossed the room and threw the door open. Josh Connelly was waiting on the other side.

"Hello," I said. "What are you doing here?"

"You have a way with words, Ali, you know that?" He looked around me into the empty room. "Can I come in?"

"Well, yes, I guess so." In all the time I'd known him, Josh had never shown up at my door before, and I couldn't help but wonder why he was there now. Probably delivering a message from Jack, I decided as I closed the door behind him.

"I see housekeeping isn't one of your strong points."

"Bitsy and I had a slight difference of opinion." I tossed the bedspread back onto the bed and began to straighten it.

"Don't tell me, you decided to settle things with your fists?"

Pretending to concentrate on fluffing the pillows, I watched the dimple deepen in his cheek. Have I ever mentioned that Josh Connelly has an almost irresistible grin?

"Close." The room *did* look as though an invading army had marched through recently. "Pillows."

"Were you the winner or the loser?"

I shot a look at the closed bathroom door where the sound of water running in the shower was clearly audible. "That's a matter of opinion, too."

"I wondered where Bitsy was," he said. "I was hoping she'd be here with you."

"I'm sure she'll be out in a minute. Or if you like, I can give her a message," I said curtly.

"That won't be necessary. Actually, you were the one I wanted to see."

"Me?"

"Yes, you." Josh smiled. "Tommy and I were thinking about getting away for a few hours and letting off some steam. We heard about a club near here that caters strictly to teenagers—good food, nonalcholic beverages and plenty of loud music. We were thinking maybe the two of you would like to come with us."

"Josh Connelly," I gasped, "are you asking me for a date?"

Too late, I realized what I had said. Good going, Anderson, I thought. So much for being cool.

"Well...yes. Sort of."

"Sort of?" I echoed suspiciously. "What does that mean?"

"It means I think the four of us could have a good time together. Besides, Tommy is dying to get together with Bitsy, and this seemed like as good a way as any to help that to happen."

"Tommy is dying to get together with Bitsy?" I cried. "You can't be serious!"

"Why not?"

"Well for one thing, he sure has a funny way of showing it."

"You know how Tommy is—he can be kind of shy."

"Tommy Meehan," I declared, "is about as shy as a Mack Truck, and you know it!"

"All right," he admitted, "he does have moments when subtlety is not his strong point."

"Moments?" I chortled. "He has days! Weeks! Years!"

"Come on, give the guy a break. He's not that bad. I know he can be a little loud sometimes, but he doesn't mean any harm. That's just how he is. This whole thing with Bitsy really has him thrown for a loop. He likes her, and he thinks she likes him, too, but he can't figure out how to make the first move."

"Oh for Pete's sake. If he'd simply open his eyes, he wouldn't have to. Bitsy's already given him just about every opening in the book. Why, just this morning she tried to offer to help him with his studies, and he cut her dead."

"Sure he did," said Josh. "It was the only thing he could do."

"What do you mean, it was the only thing he could do? It looked to me like the perfect opportunity for him to accept her offer graciously and make them both happy."

"Don't you see?" asked Josh, though it must have been perfectly obvious that I didn't. "He was embarrassed because she found out he was having trouble in school. That's why he got so mad when you blurted the whole thing out. Now he's afraid she thinks he's stupid or something.''

I started to say that anyone with any sense could see that Tommy was stupid without having to be told, but one look at the expression on Josh's face and I thought better of it. At least that explained why Tommy had been so angry earlier.

"Bitsy doesn't think Tommy's stupid," I told Josh. "She thinks he's uninterested."

Josh shot me one of his cocky grins. "Kind of like the way you feel about me, huh?''

"Yeah," I said, matching him grin for grin. "Kind of. Only in my case, it's true."

Instead of answering, Josh only laughed, confirming what I already knew. The boy had entirely too high an opinion of himself.

"Bitsy tells me you've got plenty of girls hanging around," I said. "So if you want to go out tonight, how come you're asking me?''

"Would you believe you're the only date I could get on such short notice?''

"You haven't gotten me yet." I was beginning to enjoy myself enormously.

"Oh, but I will," Josh replied, sounding to my mind, much too confident.

"Don't be so sure. I haven't decided yet whether or not I can stand a whole evening of trying to be nice to you."

"Maybe not. But I'm willing to bet that for Bitsy's sake, you'd try."

I have to admit, he had me there. "Okay," I said, "you're on. Just give me a minute to check and make sure it's all right with Bitsy."

I knocked on the door, then stuck my head inside the steamy room, yelling so that I could be heard above the running water. As I'd expected, Bitsy not only liked the idea, she was thrilled. So thrilled in fact, that her shriek of acceptance could easily be heard by Josh who was still waiting by the bed.

"Great." He strode over to the door and let himself out. "We'll be by to pick you up around seven, okay?"

"Fine. We'll be ready."

"Oh, and Ali?" He paused just outside in the hallway. "Wear something pretty, okay?"

The pillow I aimed at his head thudded harmlessly against the wooden door he pulled shut behind him.

Wear something pretty, indeed! As if I had any intention of letting Josh Connelly tell me what to wear!

But somehow, after I'd taken my own turn in the shower, then wiped the steam off the lighted mirror so that I could dab on some makeup, I found myself looking through the selection of things that were hanging in my closet and wondering just what Josh would consider pretty. Surely not the faded denims and polo shirt that I usually wore when I went out with friends? No, that was entirely too plain. So was the cotton wraparound skirt I kept on hand for emergencies.

In my mind, pretty had always meant frivolous. And with my travel wardrobe pared down to a minimum, that was just the sort of stuff I'd left at home.

"What's the matter?" asked Bitsy. She came up behind me to peer over my shoulder as I studied the contents of the closet.

"My clothes, that's what's the matter." I waved a hand disparagingly at the selection. "They're dull."

"That's funny. You never thought so before."

"Sure I did. I just never got around to doing anything about it, that's all."

"Well, as far as doing anything about it goes, you're a little late now," Bitsy pointed out. "At least, if you're worrying about what to wear tonight."

"I'm not worried at all." I pulled out the first thing that came to hand—a light blue cotton jumpsuit that I usually wore with sneakers and a T-shirt underneath. "It's only Tommy and Josh, for

Pete's sake. There's no use in dressing up for them.''

"Oh, I don't know," Bitsy drawled in her best Southern belle voice. She slipped a gauzy sundress off its hanger and over her head. "I think it's kind of nice to dress up every once in a while."

"Sure," I retorted as I struggled into my jumpsuit. "You would. It's like sipping tea on the veranda. It must be in your genes, or something."

"You're a fine one to be talking about genes," Bitsy sniffed. "After all, your ancestors were the ones who burned Atlanta."

"Not that Civil War business again." To hide my smile, I sat down on the floor and fished around under the bed where I'd thrown my sneakers earlier.

"You started it," Bitsy began, then paused as she watched me pull out my shoes and tie them on. "Good Lord, you're not wearing *those* are you?"

"Of course, why not?"

"Why anyone would take a perfectly decent jumpsuit, and then muck it up with high-top sneakers! By the time you get done, you'll look like you're all set to clean stalls!"

"Thanks a lot." It was bad enough that Bitsy had a way of pulling out any old thing and slipping it on and immediately looking gorgeous. But when she started in on what I looked like—well, that was another matter.

"Look," said Bitsy. "Do you want to borrow something of mine?"

I laughed in spite of myself. "Have you looked at the difference in our figures lately? I'd never be able to fill out your clothes."

"I know I'm too fat," she said. "But maybe if we took something and belted it—"

"Too fat! Bitsy, you've got a great figure. I know plenty of girls who would kill to look like you."

"No! Really?"

"Really. Take my word for it. You look great. Tommy won't know what hit him."

"That's what I'm hoping. Like my mama always says, when in doubt, wear pearls."

"Bitsy, you're not wearing pearls."

"Don't worry about it, it's the thought that counts." She turned to study me with a critical eye. "Now that I'm all set, let's see what we can do about you."

In no time at all, she'd replaced my sneakers with a pair of low heels. Then the jumpsuit's cotton belt was whipped off and tossed away in favor of one made of red leather. "Now we're getting somewhere," she said. "There's just one more thing…" She opened the top two buttons at the jumpsuit's neck, then pulled the collar apart.

"If you're looking for cleavage," I said, "don't bother. Besides, I liked those buttons just the way they were. I'm not looking to flash anybody, you know."

"Of course not." Bitsy crossed the room and began to rummage through her half-packed suitcase. "We're not going to leave all that open space just sitting there. I'm sure I have a scarf in here that has both red and blue in it. Aha!" she cried triumphantly, whipping out a swatch of brightly colored silk. *"Voilà!"*

"Are you sure it's me, or should I say *moi*?"

"Of course it's you. It's perfect!"

Even though it was a Monday night, the club was crowded when we arrived. Josh immediately took control, leading the way to an empty table that was in the corner of the room. It was close enough to the dance floor that we could watch the action, but still far enough away that we could hear what we were saying when we wanted to talk.

Strangely enough, Bitsy and Tommy didn't seem to have much to say. It was kind of weird. They were sitting next to each other on one side of the table, looking as awkward as two people who had just met for the first time. Josh and I felt bound to do all we could to keep the conversation rolling.

We talked about everything we could think of from baseball, to books, to Dire Straits. Our efforts to include Tommy and Bitsy in the discussion were totally in vain. But no matter what we did, they continued to sit there as stiff and as silent as a pair of wooden soldiers.

Josh and I exchanged a mystified look, then fell upon our hamburgers happily. After the last twenty minutes, it was a relief not to have to talk anymore.

By the time the meal was finished, the band had finished its break and was back on stage. As soon as they began to fiddle with their instruments, Bitsy began to wiggle in her seat. I knew just how she was feeling. Both of us loved to dance.

The band played all the way through its first song, however, and started on its second, and still neither of the boy's had made a move.

"All right," I announced, "who's going to dance with me?"

To my relief, Josh wasted no time in leaping to his feet. "I believe the honor's mine," he said, and it was all I could do to keep from giggling.

As we made our way to the dance floor, I could see Bitsy and Tommy following along behind. Probably only so they wouldn't have to talk to each other, I thought wryly.

The first couple of songs were loud and fast, the kind that didn't require anything more that a bit of bobbing and jumping up and down in place. Josh was a very good dancer. It wasn't surprising, when you stop to consider that riding, which he was also very good at, required a fair amount of coordination as well.

When the band swung into its first slow number, I decided I'd had enough. I started to walk off the dance floor back to our seats, but Josh grabbed my hand from behind and swung me back around into his arms.

"Not so fast," he said, laughing at the look of utter astonishment on my face. "We haven't finished yet."

The next thing I knew his arms had closed around me again and we were moving in time to the music. Once I got used to the idea, it was really pretty cool. The only problem was, it made me mad to think that here was yet another thing he was justified in being conceited about. As if he didn't have enough already!

After what seemed like only seconds the song ended, and we pulled apart. Across the dance floor Tommy and Bitsy were doing the same. Whereas before there'd been only silence between them, now they were talking and laughing. Bitsy was giggling at something Tommy had said, and Tommy had a big grin on his face.

At the table Bitsy paused before sitting down. "I'm going to the ladies' room," she said, glancing at me. "Want to come?"

I've never understood why boys go to the men's room one at a time, while girls visit the ladies' in groups. The only reason I could come up with was that it gave you an opportunity to compare notes on how the evening was going. Since tonight that sounded like a good idea to me, I eagerly agreed.

Leaving the boys to order some more drinks we made our way to the lounge where we sat down in front of a big, lighted mirror to freshen our make-up. Bitsy, I noted, needed no such repairs. She was positively glowing.

"It's about time," I said. "I was beginning to think you two were never going to loosen up."

"Me, too," Bitsy admitted. "Things started out okay, but then Tommy was so quiet after we got here, I was afraid maybe he was sorry he'd ever asked me out at all."

"So?" I asked. "How did you break the ice?"

"I stepped on his foot," Bitsy confided with a low giggle. "I mean, really mashed it. He'll probably be sore for a week."

"How did that help?"

"Well, first it gave me a chance to be ever so apologetic. Then it gave him a chance to be chivalrous in return. Believe it or not, he actually rose to the occasion."

"Tommy Meehan? Mr. Bad Manners himself?"

"Sure. First he tried to tell me that the whole thing was his fault. Then, when I insisted that I really was all feet, he offered to teach me how to dance. Of course, that involved holding me a little closer than usual, and then we just sort of took it from there."

"So I noticed. But I seem to remember you telling me once that your mama made you go to charm school. Didn't anyone there ever get around to teaching you the fine art of dancing?"

"What do you think?" she asked.

Chapter Five

As horse shows go, Fairfield is one of the nicest. The courses are big and well spread out, with none of the tricky corners and tight turns that trip you up at other shows. Besides that, the event is held at a country club and, for the five days it lasts, the club facilities—a swimming pool and tennis court—are open to the exhibitors as well.

The long, sprawling outside course is custom-made for my style of riding, and Fairfield is one of those shows where I can usually count on doing well. This time, however, nothing seemed to go right. Instead of attacking the fences with his usual zeal, Dare Me was tentative and unsure, at times even downright pokey.

At a "C" or even a "B" level show, it might not have made a difference, but here the competition was top notch. Any mistake at all was one too many. By the time the weekend arrived, Bitsy and Blithe Spirit were ahead in points in the large junior hunter division, while Josh and Tommy were cleaning up with their jumpers.

Everybody was winning, I thought, feeling terribly sorry for myself as I wandered idly through the concession stands between classes. Everybody but me.

"Hey, Ali!"

I looked up to find Pete hurrying toward me. Since it's unusual for my brother to do anything quickly, I figured this had to be something important.

"Jack wants to see you. He sent me out to hunt you down. It sounds like trouble to me," he added with more relish than sympathy. "What did you do now?"

I had my own suspicions about why Jack might want to see me, but I sure wasn't about to confide them to my brother.

A request from Jack was roughly the equivalent of a royal summons, and I set off immediately for the stabling area. I found Jack there, putting the finishing touches on the braid job of a working hunter that was showing that afternoon.

"Have a seat." He gestured toward a bale of hay on the side of the aisle. "You're going to be here awhile."

I watched Jack's fingers move deftly down the horse's neck as he spoke around the long darning needle clutched between his teeth.

"I want to know what's wrong," he said bluntly. "Your rounds this whole week haven't been worth spit. You don't even have so much as a green ribbon yet, do you?"

I shook my head.

"So?"

"I don't know. You've been watching all week. Have I really been riding that badly?"

"Technically, no. You're still judging your fences well, but your performance seems to have lost some zip. It's a long course, Alex, maybe longer than you're used to. He's going to sleep on you out there. Sometimes I think the snow's going to fly before the two of you make it back in."

"I know what you mean. But I swear, Jack, I don't think it's me. Dare Me's gone really doggy on me."

Jack fixed me with a cool stare. "Are you giving him enough leg?"

"Leg? Jack, I'm using everything I've got! I even tried spurs on him yesterday, and that didn't help."

"Hmmm." Jack frowned thoughtfully. "He isn't off his feed, is he?"

"No."

"Sore anywhere?"

"Not that I can tell."

"I hate to say this, but different horses age at different speeds. It could be he's simply beginning to feel old."

The thought had occurred to me, too, but like the ostrich with its head in the sand, I'd decided that if I didn't think about the problem, it couldn't possibly be true. "What do you think I should do?"

"For one thing, start working him less, effective immediately. No more of those early-morning hacks cross-country, and as little schooling as possible between classes. Maybe if we lay off him a little, he'll come back to us."

Jack reached down and patted my shoulder awkwardly. "Don't worry," he said. "I'd be willing to bet that old guy still has more than a few good years left in him."

"I hope so." Dare Me was my friend, my companion. Where would I be without him?

To my relief, Jack's advice proved to be if not an instant cure-all, at least a step in the right direction. With less work, Dare Me's performance improved, and on Saturday morning, we were even able to pull a third in the Medal, behind Josh, who won it, and ahead of Bitsy, who placed fifth.

In the Maclay, it was Tommy's turn to shine as he and Lobo turned in the winning trip to pick up his third blue and qualify for the finals at the Garden in November.

"Congratulations," I said, giving him a big grin as I rode out of the ring behind him, the fourth place white ribbon hanging from Dare Me's bridle. "That's really terrific."

"It is, isn't it?" Tommy looked thoroughly pleased with himself.

"Hey!" cried Josh, as he and Bitsy rode up beside us. "Give the rest of us a chance. We want to go to the finals too."

"Well yeah, sure..." said Tommy, suddenly uncertain. "Of course, you do. You will." He glanced around at the three of us. "We all will."

After returning the horses to their stalls, the four of us walked over to the club snack bar and got some lunch. Now that Tommy and Bitsy seemed to be pretty well established as a couple, Josh and I were doing more things together too. It was only natural, I guess, since Bitsy was my best friend, and Tommy, his.

Although it pained me to admit it, the better I got to know Josh, the more things I found to like about him.

Over lunch, the talk turned to the exhibitors' ball that the Fairfield Hunt Club was hosting that evening. Usually Bitsy and I skipped things like that since most of the people who went tended to be part of an older crowd. Now, however, Tommy, who was in high spirits over his win, declared the ball to be his victory celebration.

"What do you say?" he asked Bitsy. "You will go with me, won't you?"

"Oh, let me see..." Bitsy consulted her watch. "Only eight hours notice? I'll have to check my calendar."

"That means yes," Tommy said confidently.

"How about you?" Josh asked me. "Is your calendar empty as well?"

"Gee, I don't know," I said, holding back a smile. "It would mean passing up *Love Boat*..."

Next thing I knew, the plans were all made, and they had arranged to pick us up in our room at the motel at eight o'clock that evening. It wasn't until we'd finished eating, then gotten up to head back to the barns, that I realized what a bind I was in.

"Bitsy," I whispered, mindful of the boys who were walking several steps behind us. "What am I going to do? You know what my clothes look like. I haven't got a single thing to wear!"

"What's the big deal? We'll just go shopping and buy you something."

My heart sank down to my toes. I hated to go shopping. Nothing I tried on ever looked right. Usually I just tried to get by in jeans and slacks and wraparound skirts—anything that didn't require trying on.

"Meet me back at the barn after your last class," Bitsy said, about to go in search of her mount for the pony classes. "In the meantime I'll check around and find out what stores are in the area. We'll find you something fabulous."

With unerring instinct Bitsy walked straight to the right department in Bloomingdale's. I followed along behind as she strode from rack to rack, picking and choosing through hundreds of dresses until she had gathered an armload that she felt merited trying on.

"All of those?" I asked faintly. The colorful array of silks and satins and chiffons which spilled off their hangers as Bitsy draped them over the chair in the dressing room, was enough to give anybody pause.

"Like my mama always says," said Bitsy, "there's no use in buying the pig until you've tasted some of the bacon. Now hurry up and get out of those jeans. You're wasting time just standing there."

No sooner had I stripped down to my underwear than Bitsy was dropping the first selection over my head.

Together we grimaced into the mirror at the way the purple chiffon clashed with my hair. "Sorry," she said. "I guess I had my coloring in mind when I chose that one. All right then, out of that one and into the next."

"This'll never work," I muttered. "I'm just not the clotheshorse type."

"Nonsense!" cried Bitsy, as she tossed aside the chiffon and zipped me into a dark blue crepe. "You've told yourself that so many times, you've actually begun to believe it. When was the last time you even tried buying something besides jeans?"

"I buy new breeches and ratcatchers all the time."

"That's not the same, and you know it." She grasped me by the shoulders and twirled me around so I faced the mirror. "There now, you see?" Stepping away, she studied the image critically. "That's not half bad at all."

"Do you really think so?" I asked, squinting at my reflection. It was certainly a big improvement over the purple chiffon, anyone could see that. But did it actually look good?

"Of course," Bitsy said. "I wouldn't say so if it didn't. The color's perfect with your eyes."

"Terrific, I'll take it."

"Oh no you don't!" cried Bitsy. "We've only just begun. You've got twelve more to try on before you set one foot outside this dressing room!" She buttoned me into her next choice, a skimpy looking yellow satin.

"Good grief!" I gulped, when I saw what I looked like in the mirror. "Definitely too much of me outside the dress, and not enough in." On we went to number four.

Over my very vocal protests, we worked our way slowly through the huge pile. Two dresses from the bottom, I pulled on a deceptively simple silver-gray silk. It was soft and swingy and flowing, and I knew right away that I had found my dress.

"That," said Bitsy with obvious satisfaction, "is what we've been looking for. The color's perfect on you, and the style's fantastic."

The funny thing was, seeing myself standing in the mirror like that, it didn't look like me at all. Studying my image critically, I could see that there was another side to me that I'd never even guessed at. A side that liked the way I looked in that dress and couldn't wait to see if Josh Connelly felt the same way. To tell the truth, it was a little bit unnerving, kind of like going for a walk under a full moon and finding yourself turning into a werewolf.

"Not everyone could carry that dress, you know," Bitsy told me. "I sure couldn't. On me, it would look like a big gray gunny sack. It needs someone tall and thin, with a figure like a fashion model."

"Built like a breadstick, you mean," I said, slipping off the dress.

Bitsy left me to pay for the purchase and ran on ahead to the shoe department. By the time I got there, she'd already made her selection. All I had to do was slip in my feet and give my approval.

"Two straps and a sole." I grumbled, when I turned them over and saw the price. I couldn't help observing that they cost just about the same as a really good pair of sneakers.

"Does it ever occur to you how much easier boys have things than girls do?" Bitsy asked later that evening as we were getting ready.

"All the time," I said. I'd only been tottering around in my new shoes for two seconds, but already I knew that by the end of the night, I was going to be in pain. "All they have to do is pull out any old suit, slap on a shirt and tie, and they're dressed. They never have to go shopping at the last minute...."

"Or be blinded by mascara that gets into their eyes," Bitsy interjected.

"Or break in a new pair of high heels by dancing in them for hours."

"Or burn their fingers setting their hair only to have it flop half an hour later."

Bitsy and I looked at each other. "Gee," she said, "we've really got it rough, haven't we?"

"Do you think we ought to dump the guys in protest?"

"Not on your life!"

The main dining room of the Hunt Club had been transformed into a setting that looked as though it might have been lifted straight from a fairy tale. Men in dark suits twirled women wearing long, colorful dresses around the dance floor. Overhead lights glinted off a shimmering ice sculpture of a horse dominating a buffet table set up on one side of the room. A twelve-piece orchestra was playing music that made me itch to get out there and do some dancing myself.

"Wow," I said, breathing the word softly under my breath. I didn't think Josh would hear me, but he did.

"I know what you mean." For what was probably the first time in his life, he looked a little intimidated. "This is something else, isn't it?"

Then some friends at a big round table near the door stood up and waved for us to join them, and suddenly everything was all right. We moved into the room and became part of the swirling crowd ourselves.

After his brief hesitation at the door, I could tell that Josh began to feel at home almost immediately. He found us seats at a table and went to get some drinks. Then, when he returned and the band struck up a new number, we were among the first out on the dance floor.

"You look happy tonight," he said, twirling me around in time to the Glenn Miller forties music.

"I am. I'm having a wonderful time."

"Should I take that personally, or do you just like swing music?"

"A little of both," I told him. Since I'm usually not the type to flirt, I almost didn't recognize myself. But tonight, anything seemed possible.

When the number finished, we went back to reclaim our seats. As ours was the only table in the room with teenagers, any new arrivals gravitated there instinctively. In our absence, the group had grown to more than a dozen.

In a way, my being with Josh almost wasn't like being on a date at all. Which was too bad, I decided, because I was beginning to think that Josh might be the kind of boy I wouldn't mind dating at all. Especially the way he looked, dark and handsome in a charcoal-gray suit. Apparently I wasn't the only one who was impressed, because I noticed some of the other girls giving me these envious little glares when they thought I wasn't looking. I have to tell you, that made me feel pretty good.

The band played until one o'clock in the morning, and we stayed until the players started packing up their instruments. "Don't anybody dare tell Jack what time we got in," Bitsy said in the car on the way back to the motel. "He'd kill us for sure."

"I wouldn't put it past him to have posted guards to check up on us," said Josh. He leaned out the window and pointed toward an old man standing on a street corner. "There, that looks like one now!"

"Do you really think so?" Bitsy asked.

Tommy, who was driving, broke up. "Are all Southern girls so gullible?" he asked. "Or is it just you?"

Watching Tommy and Bitsy together had made me realize how much better they were getting along these days. I remembered how Josh had only started asking me out in the first place because he thought Tommy needed some moral support. Now I couldn't help but wonder where we stood.

When we reached the motel, Tommy and Bitsy paused by the car. Josh and I walked on ahead to give them some privacy. Josh waited while I unlocked the door. Having him stand so close made me kind of jumpy so I decided maybe I ought to ask him what I had been thinking about and see what he had to say.

"You know..." I said, then stopped to clear my throat.

"Yes?" I realized that, for a boy, he had the greatest eyelashes I'd ever seen—all long, and thick, and dark. I'd never even noticed them before. Now I couldn't seem to look anywhere else.

"I was thinking," I began again. "Now that Bitsy and Tommy seem to be getting along so well, I guess you and I don't have to keep them company anymore. I mean, that is why you asked me out isn't it?"

It was a moment before Josh spoke, but when he did, he was smiling. Not that cocky smile that gets on my nerves, but a real honest-to-goodness smile that warmed up his whole face. "I didn't ask you out to please Tommy and Bitsy," he said.

Chapter Six

On Sunday, the Fairfield show ended. Monday, we moved to upstate New York, the next location in the cycle of competition that would continue on through the fall. After New York, it was Vermont, and after Vermont, Rhode Island. One by one, the wins we needed slowly began to pile up. By the time we reached the Branchville show which was held in conjunction with a country fair in early August, Josh had qualified for the Medal, and Bitsy and I had each picked up two more wins.

In fact, for the most part, everything seemed to be going pretty well. I would have been more enthusiastic, except that I was still having some problems with Dare Me. For a while, working him less seemed to do the trick. When I rode him in the classes, he felt almost like his old self. As time passed, however, he gradually began to worsen again, and Jack started talking about bringing in a vet and having him thoroughly checked out.

Still and all, we'd had two more wins. Blithe was going great guns and Bitsy hadn't done any better than I had. Maybe I was simply expecting too much of Dare Me. When a niggling voice deep inside insisted that he'd always lived up to my expectations before, I shut it out and refused to listen.

Needless to say, with all this going on, I'd been pretty preoccupied. As a result, I'd hardly seen anything of Josh. And that was beginning to make me mad. I mean, okay so I wasn't going out of my way to find him, but he sure wasn't knocking down any doors on my account either.

That was the trouble with boys, I decided. They were inconsistent. Interested one day, and cool the next. Not that I'd been acting any different, I supposed, but at least with Dare Me's problems to think about I had a good reason. As far as I could see, Josh didn't have any excuse.

Bitsy, meanwhile, was spending almost all her free time with Tommy. She always tried to include me whenever they had plans, but now that my presence was no longer needed, I didn't particularly like the idea of tagging along like an afterthought. Besides, with the worrying I'd been doing lately, I couldn't quite summon up the same carefree mood that was needed to match theirs.

From what Bitsy told me, Josh often went out with them. She mentioned that he'd been asking where I was. But as time passed and I continued ducking out on the excursions, the questions stopped.

Between that and everything else that was going on, I had plenty to brood about. Which is why when Josh rode past on China Doll, looking supremely confident, I wasn't feeling in a particularly chatty mood.

Why was everything always so easy for him? Didn't he ever have to work like we mere mortals to make things come out right? Not only had he been beating me regularly in the equitation classes, but I'd heard from Jack that China Doll was now leading the country in the point standings for the year-end jumper title. As if that wasn't enough, Bitsy had told me that thanks to Josh's coaching, Tommy had breezed through his make-up course with a solid B.

All their lives seemed so together. I was thrilled for them, I told myself determinedly. So why wasn't I happier?

"Good luck," Josh called, touching his crop to the brim of his black velvet hat in a jaunty salute. Then he grinned in that way he had and I could almost guess what his next words would be. "You'll need it if you think you're going to beat me. Don't look now, but China Doll and I are hot!"

"Is that so?"

Now that I'd gotten to know Josh better, I realized all that surface cockiness was just that, on the surface. Once you got past it, there were times when he was a genuinely nice person. Then again, I remembered with a sigh, there were still times when he got on my nerves. One thing I had to admit though. When Josh was around, life was never dull.

"Pity," I said, returning his jibe with one of my own. "The word I got from Jack was that this judge likes a nice, calm cool performance."

"Touché! In that case, you shouldn't have any trouble."

"Believe me, I'm not planning to."

For a moment, Josh simply sat there and studied me with a quizzical look on his face. "You know, Ali," he said finally, "you don't make things easy."

"I should hope not," I said firmly. "If I can't beat you now, I'll be in big trouble come November."

"Is that all you ever think about, beating me?"

Something about his tone made me stop and look, really look, at him. It was probably the first time I had done so since the night we went to the ball at the Fairfield show.

"No," I said as Dare Me shifted restlessly beneath me. "I think about lots of things. But unfortunately, right now most of them aren't very good."

Josh opened his mouth to say something, but at that moment Bitsy and Tommy rode up, with Jack following along on foot behind them.

"What are you doing just standing around?" Jack bellowed. "Get those animals moving. You two are supposed to be warming up, not just taking up space!"

Automatically we moved away to do as we were told. Jack set up some practice fences and put us through our paces. Dare Me seemed to be feeling pretty good and my confidence grew as I wondered whether today might be my day to pick up that elusive third Maclay that would qualify me for the Garden.

As things turned out, it might have been, because I came awfully close. Dare Me was fit, and full of himself. For the first time in a long time, we were totally in sync, working together like the polished team we'd been in the spring. I thought we had the class in the bag until I saw Josh's round and knew that was what I had to beat.

When the numbers were called for the riders to return to the ring for the ride-off, he and I were one and two. Then came time to switch mounts and I ended up on a beautifully trained chestnut Thoroughbred. I had to bite back a giggle when I saw Josh climbing aboard a stocky little pinto that didn't look as though it even belonged in the class at all.

My second round was smooth and neat, and I knew that the judges couldn't help but be impressed. Feeling pretty good, I rode out of the ring, then pulled up beside the gate to watch Josh. A quick glance confirmed that the pinto he'd drawn lacked everything from talent to finesse. Yet somehow Josh succeeded in making the little horse perform like a champion. When he rode out of the ring, the applause that followed him was long and hard.

The judges announced their decision. The blue ribbon went to Josh, and I had to be content with the red. Willing back tears of disappointment, I accepted the ribbon from the ringmaster and thanked him with a smile. As I followed Josh out of the ring, I glared at the regal bearing of his broad back.

Big deal, I thought, so Josh Connelly had gotten lucky again. What else was new?

I returned my mount to Pete's capable hands. "Tough luck," he said, taking the reins as I hopped down and ran up my stirrups. "But you have to admit, Josh did a heck of a job with that pinto. Who'd have thought that horse ever would have been able to jump like that? I'll say one thing for Josh—he sure can ride."

Pete headed back to the stables, and I stopped by one of the concessions to pick up a can of cold soda. Then, with nothing else to do for the afternoon, I wandered out to the small outer barns for a look around.

Not surprisingly, the bleachers were almost empty. Clutching my soda, I climbed the steep steps and settled in the top tier. From there, I had a pretty good view of the rest of the fairground which included everything from a busy midway to a soaring roller coaster.

I wondered what Bitsy was up to. Off somewhere with Tommy, no doubt.

"Hey, you up there!"

Startled from my thoughts, I looked down and saw Josh standing on the ground behind the bleachers. I gave him a half-hearted wave.

"I've been looking everywhere for you," he called. "Stay there, I'm coming up."

Stay there? What did he think I was going to do, fly off the railing and into the clouds?

The steep climb hadn't even left him winded I noted as Josh mounted the last step and sat down beside me.

"What are you doing up here all by yourself?"

"Thinking," I replied shortly, hoping that might shut him up.

"I looked for you after the Maclay. I wanted to tell you how sorry I was that it had to come down to the two of us like that. You and Dare Me looked great—"

"Yeah, sure. Be magnanimous. You can afford to be. You were the winner."

"But that doesn't mean you didn't ride well—"

"Only that you rode better," I interrupted him. "Is that what you were going to say?" I knew that I was being obnoxious, but somehow I couldn't seem to help myself. I'd wanted that blue ribbon so badly that I could almost taste it.

"Not exactly. I was going to say that it was a stroke of luck I drew a horse that allowed me to show off more talent than the horse that you were assigned to did."

"Luck? Well I guess I shouldn't be surprised. You've always had plenty of that!"

"Not always. Just because sometimes I'm able to make things look easy doesn't mean I don't have to work for them just as hard as everybody else."

"Téll me about it," I muttered. In my present mood, I wasn't about to give an inch.

"I might," Josh said slowly. "If I thought you were interested. But from where I sit it looks as though the only thing you *are* interested in is mooching around here feeling sorry for yourself."

"A lot you know!" I cried, leaping to my feet. The fact that he was right only made me madder still. "I am not feeling sorry for myself."

"Sure. I'll bet you've always liked to go off by yourself and sulk. Probably ever since you were a little girl."

"Cut it out!" I snapped.

"Come on," he said, patting the seat beside him. "Sit. I know how you feel. You're not the only one who feels the pressure around here. Sometimes, I begin to think that if I don't win, it'll be the end of the world. That's when I know I'm starting to crack up."

"What do you do about it?" Josh always looked so calm and in control, it was hard to imagine that he ever had moments of self-doubt.

"If I can, I just climb on the Doll and go for a long ride. I try to remember that the horses and the riding are what it's supposed to be all about. Not the winning."

"I used to do that. But I can't anymore. Dare Me's been off his form lately, and Jack said maybe he was getting too much work. He turned fifteen this year. I hate to even think about it, but I guess he's getting old.''

Josh looked surprised. ''Fifteen isn't that old,'' he said. ''There've been plenty of horses who have shown to that age, and beyond.''

''I know. Jack thinks we ought to call in a vet, and get him a complete examination.''

''You should. Why haven't you?''

''Do you want the truth?''

Josh nodded.

''Because I'm afraid of what they'll find. I'm afraid it will be like the cat I had when I was younger. We dropped her off at the vet one day because she wasn't feeling well, and the next day she was dead. I never even found out what she died of. I know it's silly, but I just keep thinking that as long as the vet doesn't have to be involved, things can't really be that bad.''

''But they are that bad. You said yourself he's been off his form. No wonder your own performances haven't been up to par.''

''Don't start making excuses for me,'' I said sharply.

''They're not called excuses when there really is a problem. Call in a vet, Ali. You need to find out what's wrong.''

I drew in my breath, then expelled it in a long sigh. He was right, and I knew it. Even just admitting that to myself seemed to lift a great weight off my shoulders.

"I guess it has to be done," I said. "I'll talk to Jack tomorrow and see about getting in a vet as soon as possible."

"Good. Believe me, no matter what he turns up, it's always better to know."

I can't say that I believed him, but the decision was made, and I knew it was the right one.

"Hey," said Josh, standing up. "I've got a great idea. Now that the show's over for the day, what do you say we take in the fair?"

"Just the two of us?"

Josh grinned. "Do you see anybody else?"

"No, I guess not."

"Come on, then." He grabbed my hand and pulled me to my feet. "This'll be fun."

Together we made our way down from the empty bleachers. We stopped at the tack room only long enough to change our clothes and then hurried on to the fairground.

As it was Saturday night, the fair was crowded. Bright lights filled the sky, illuminating a host of enticing rides. Barkers lined the midway, extolling the virtues of their booths which offered everything from pitch-and-toss to target practice. Underneath the dark, starry sky, the fair looked almost magical.

"Which shall it be first?" asked Josh, stopping just inside the entrance. "The rides, or the midway?"

"The midway, I think. I hate to admit it, but I have a terrible weakness for cotton candy."

"I'm a candied-apple man myself," said Josh. He took my hand and led the way to a stand that offered both. "What do you say we skip dinner and simply eat our way from one end of the fair to the other?"

We made our way slowly down the concession-lined avenue that formed the center of the attractions.

At the frog hop, Josh won a black-and-white panda, which he presented to me graciously.

"But this is yours," I protested, putting it back in his hands. "You're the one who won it."

"That's all right," said Josh. "I want you to have it. What would I do with a panda?"

"I see what you mean. I guess having a stuffed animal on your bed wouldn't do much for the great Josh Connelly's image. Think of your reputation!"

"Hah!" Josh cried, then paused. "What reputation?"

"If you don't know, I'm not going to be the one to tell you."

"Know what?" Josh prodded, but I turned and started walking away toward the booth where tickets for the rides were being sold. "Know what?"

"Hmm," I said, ignoring him as I studied the prices on the board. "Give us two for the roller coaster and two for the ferris wheel, please."

"Alexandra Anderson, if you don't talk to me, you are going to be sorry!"

"Oh for Pete's sake," I said, as the ferris wheel stopped and we were handed into our seats. "Don't get all bent out of shape. You must know what I meant. Everybody's talking about it."

"About what?"

"About the fact that you're a cinch to be invited down to Gladstone in the spring for the next U.S.E.T. screening trials. Everybody says so. I even heard Jack talking about it the other day."

"Even Jack?" said Josh. Now he sounded impressed. We both knew that Jack was not the sort to engage in idle gossip. "That's all I've ever wanted for years. I sure hope he knows what he was talking about."

"He usually does," I said as the ferris wheel started with a rough jerk, and we went flying upward through the cool night air. Around and around the big wheel went. I snuggled up next to

Josh. He reached out and put his arm around me. I sighed as I leaned down and rested my head on his shoulder. It was a relief to be able to have fun, to go out and forget all about my problems, even if it was only for a little while.

Chapter Seven

The next day we moved again, this time to Monmouth in southern New Jersey. By the time a vet finally arrived to check Dare Me out, it was Tuesday afternoon.

"This horse is about to pop a splint," he explained, crouching down beside Dare Me's front leg. He ran a hand over the cannon bone. "I can feel it here, right under the skin."

"A splint?" Jack's brow furrowed. "Those are for young horses. This gelding's fifteen years old."

"I can't help that." The vet stood up and wiped his hands on the back of his pants. "Apparently nobody's let him in on the fact that he should have gotten this out of the way years ago. Besides, any sort of stress or strain can cause a flare-up." He looked out over the show ground at the horses that were being ridden around the field. "You'd be amazed how many horses on the circuit have them."

I listened to everything the vet had to say about causes and treatments, and none of it sounded encouraging. Jack just kept nodding his head the whole time, so it was hard to tell which of the various options he actually agreed with. When I asked him about it afterward, all he said was that since the horse was mine, it was going to have to be my decision.

That evening, back at the motel, I sat Bitsy down and told her the story.

"A splint?" she interrupted, when I'd barely gotten started. "At his age? What did the vet say?"

"It's a little extra piece of bone on the foreleg," I explained. "Sometimes when the leg is stressed, the ligaments that hold it in place stretch, and it pops out. That's why Dare Me hasn't been himself lately. His leg was giving him trouble. The vet said that the splint is just about to pop and that when it does, he'll be lame for a couple of weeks, maybe even longer."

"That's terrible," Bitsy cried. "Can't you do anything?"

"That's just it," I said. "There are several things I can do, but none of them are particularly appealing."

"Hmm." Bitsy frowned as she flopped down on the bed. I could see that she was settling in for the duration. "Tell me what your options are, and let's see if we can figure out which one's the best."

"I don't think there is a best one. But here they are. The vet said the only thing that is going to heal the splint is time. Ideally Dare Me should be kept out of work for the entire period he's lame, no matter how long it takes—"

"But if you do that, you're going to miss out on the fall shows! Even if Dare Me is back in training in November, you won't have qualified to ride in the finals."

"I know. That's the first thing that occurred to me too. Jack says there is another alternative, although it's not a very pleasant one. After the vet left, he and I discussed the possibility of using butazolidin."

"That's a painkiller, right?"

"A very widely used one, although it isn't approved for use by the A.H.S.A. If we decided to go that way, it would be possible for me to keep showing Dare Me—he'd still have the pain, he just wouldn't know it. The splint would take longer to heal, but as long as we were very careful, it shouldn't cause any permanent damage. Then after the finals in November, he could have the rest of the winter off to recuperate."

"What do you mean it *shouldn't* cause permanent damage?"

"Jack doesn't know for sure. He says I should definitely be aware that there is a risk involved."

"That's not the only risk," Bitsy pointed out. "I've seen horses that are shown on bute. Sally Burnham's mare, Larkspur, for one. Remember her? Everybody said she was doped to the gills, and she was always knocking things down.

"Bute's not only bad for the horse, it can be dangerous for the rider as well," she added. "How does a horse who's numb from the knee down know whether or not it's hit a fence? The way I hear it, some of the worst falls are caused by that stuff."

"You're not telling me anything I don't already know," I said grimly. "But what choice do I really have? Right now I've got four wins. I'm one short in both the Medal and the Maclay. It's not as if I can rest Dare Me now and hope he'll be ready for the finals later on, because even if he is, *I* won't be qualified."

"What if you try pulling him out for a month?" Bitsy suggested. "Say until the middle of September. Then, if that doesn't work, maybe you could try pinfiring him."

"I don't have that kind of time." I felt myself growing cold all over, frustration turning into raw fear—fear that all my plans for the future were falling apart before I'd even had a chance to try and make them work.

Before I'd sat down and talked to Bitsy, I'd almost been able to fool myself into thinking that things really weren't so bad. But now that we'd laid out all the alternatives, I was forced to accept the truth—that everything I'd worked so hard for during the last six years might be about to go up in smoke.

Like Josh and most of the other kids who rode equitation on the circuit, my goal had always been to win a spot on the U.S. Equestrian Team. I hoped to represent the United States in international competition and maybe even, if I was lucky, the Olympics. Traditionally, the Medal, the Maclay, and the U.S.E.T. class have been the proving ground for future team members. Throughout the year, the junior riders are watched and rated and the best are selected to go to Gladstone, N.J. where the screening trials take place each spring.

Since I was already sixteen, that meant I only had one more year after this one in which to compete. Taking several months off now would prove disastrous to my plans. Already I was making things harder on myself by skipping portions of the circuit to attend school. After a setback like this, I might well be finished.

"What other choice do you really have?" asked Bitsy. "Think about what could happen if you decide to keep Dare Me in training. You might qualify, but there's no guarantee that he won't break down between now and November anyway. Then where would you be?"

"About the same place I am now—up the creek without a paddle."

"Besides, you said it yourself. That drug hasn't been approved by the A.H.S.A."

"That doesn't stop half the stables on the circuit from using it anyway."

"Just because they do, doesn't mean you should."

"I know." I let out a long, weary sigh. "Normally I wouldn't even consider such a thing. But now I just don't know what to do. No matter how I look at it, the whole situation seems impossible."

"My mama has this saying," Bitsy began and I groaned.

When she didn't finish, I felt contrite. I could see from the expression on her face that she had heard my groan, and that it had hurt her feelings. "Tell me," I said, "what does your mother have to say about a situation like this?"

"She would say," Bitsy recited in her soft drawl, "that when your date goes nose first into the punch bowl, it's time to come home from the ball."

Down as I was, I couldn't help but laugh. "Let's hope I haven't quite reached that point yet!"

"Do you want to know what else my mama always says?"

"Sure."

"She says it's a whole lot better to change your plans than to lose them altogether."

The next few days were some of the worst that I have ever spent. I climbed on Dare Me the following morning thinking that he might at least be fit for one more week, only to discover that his condition was now far enough advanced to make riding the course, much less winning a class, impossible.

Jack was sympathetic to my plight but, as always, business came first. He needed a decision, he told me, and as soon as possible. If Dare Me was not going to be shown, he wanted him sent home so he could bring in one of his other horses and put the stall space to better use.

Over the next several days, I heard a variety of opinions as to what I should do. From everyone.

Everyone, that is, except Josh, who offered no opinion whatsoever. But while he remained silent, his best friend Tommy was, as usual, extremely vocal. I should use the bute, he said, and hope for the best. The majority of the other riders agreed.

It was so easy for them to decide. Why was I the only one who couldn't make up my mind?

Finally, on Friday afternoon, I went to seek Josh out. I needed somebody to talk to, someone who was mature, and levelheaded, and most of all, objective. The thought crossed my mind how much my opinion of him had changed as the summer had progressed. In the spring, I would never have even considered him in the role of a confidant. Now I couldn't think of anybody better.

Tommy had just won the Medal class, his first, and he and Josh were standing at ringside, talking excitedly. I hung back for a minute, not wanting to interrupt. But then Josh noticed me standing there, excused himself and came over to say hello.

"I've been looking for you," I said, as he approached.

"Well, that's a switch," Josh said in an odd tone. Then he grinned teasingly and everything was all right. "Did you want something in particular, or were you just looking to feast your eyes on a bit of male pulchritude?"

"Pulchritude?" I repeated with a snort. "Where do you come up with these words anyway?"

"Tommy feeds them to me," said Josh. "Why did you want to see me?" He looped an arm casually around my shoulder as we began to walk around the large show ground.

"It's about Dare Me," I said. "Everybody else seems to have an opinion except you. I was wondering what you think."

"What I think," Josh said, "is that I ought to stay out of this. It's your decision, Ali. There's no way I'm going to make it for you."

"I'm not asking you to make if for me! All I'm asking for is a little advice."

"From where I sit, it seems to me that you've had plenty of advice already. Everybody at Jack's is speculating as to what you're going to do."

"I know they are, and believe me it doesn't make things any easier. The problem is, I've only got two choices. One's bad, and the other's worse."

"You've got that right," said Josh. "Now which one are you going to choose?"

"What would you do if it was China Doll who was in trouble?"

"That's not a fair question. And you know it. I can't put myself in your shoes, and thank God I don't have to. I'd like to think I'd do the right thing, but to tell you the truth, I'm not sure."

"The right thing, the right thing!" I cried. "Everybody's talking about doing the right thing. The problem is, I don't know what that is!"

"All right," he said. "Let's lay out the facts. Fact one: it's in your best interests to keep Dare Me on the circuit. Fact two: the only way to accomplish that is by using bute. Fact three: bute is not only dangerous, but also illegal—"

"When you put it that way, you make me sound like a real jerk for even considering it."

"Don't," Josh interrupted me. "Anyone in your shoes would be thinking along the same lines. Don't kid yourself, Ali. The circuit may have its moments, but nobody's here to have a good time. We all came to win, and that's the bottom line."

"But what if the cost of winning is simply too high?"

Josh shrugged. "That's a decision only you can make." He grasped my shoulders and turned me toward him. "It's your life, Ali," he said seriously. "You know what you ought to do, and you know what you want to do. But you're the only one who can decide what you're going to do."

"Thanks a lot." I snapped. My anger was unreasonable, and I knew it as well as anybody. There was no easy solution. Why had I been so sure that talking to Josh would make a difference? "You've been a big help." I turned on my heel and began to walk away.

"I dare you, Ali!" Josh called after me. I stopped and spun in my tracks.

"You dare me to do what, Josh Connelly?"

"I dare you to do what's right!"

"Right for whom?" I demanded. "Right for me? Right for the horse? Or maybe—" even knowing that I shouldn't, I was still angry enough to fling the words out "—right for someone who'd like to see some of the competition get out of the way?"

"If that's what you really think, then there's nothing more we have to say to each other." As I watched, he strode back down the hill, his anger obvious in everything from the stiff set of his shoulders to the jerky motion of his stride.

"I've really done it now," I told Bitsy later that night. We were in the motel restaurant eating what could only be described as a rather marginal-tasting dinner. "Josh will probably never speak to me again."

"After the things you said to him, no wonder." Bitsy looked down at her plate disgustedly. The menu called it the diet special, and it contained several carrot sticks, an unappetizing looking chopped sirloin patty, and enough cottage cheese to choke a horse.

"Here," I said, lifting my plate and switching it for hers. "I'm not eating anyway. What difference does it make if I don't eat a hot roast beef sandwich with mashed potatoes and gravy, or a diet special that even a rabbit wouldn't touch?"

Ignoring her protests, I set down the plate in front of her, then had the satisfaction of watching her tuck into my meal.

"It wasn't that I was mad at him exactly," I explained. "It was more life in general that was getting me down. The problem was that Josh got in the way. And when he refused to help me out—"

"You mean when he refused to tell you what to do," Bitsy interrupted, talking around a mouthful of mashed potatoes. "After all, from what you've told me, he did try to help. He laid out all your options for you so that you could see clearly what they were, then left the final decision up to you."

Bitsy paused for another large bite, before going on with her lecture. "If I didn't consider myself entitled as your best friend, and if I didn't enjoy meddling so much, it's exactly the same thing I would have done. In fact," she added, "now that I think about it, it's probably what I should have done."

"Don't be silly. You know I wanted to hear your opinion. Just the way I wanted to hear Josh's. After all, I asked him for it, didn't I?"

"It doesn't sound to me that you asked him any-thing. More likely you told him what you wanted, then yelled at him when he didn't give it to you."

"Well . . . maybe you have a point—"

"Maybe? Are you serious?"

"All right, so you *do* have a point. There, now are you satisfied?"

"Totally." She glanced at me speculatively. "Now that that's out of the way, have you made a decision yet about what you are going to do?"

"I guess so," I said slowly. The image of Josh Connelly standing on that hill, daring me to do the right thing, floated before my eyes. I pushed it away. "I haven't told anybody, not even Jack. I figured there'd be time enough to find him tomor-row and let him know. On Monday, when the rest of you are moving to C.W. Post, Dare Me and Pete and I will be going home."

"Oh, Alex," Bitsy's green eyes clouded with tears. "I'm really sorry. Even though I think it's for the best, I still feel awful. I'm going to miss you terribly."

"I guess my parents will be glad. They're always saying they don't see enough of us."

"But it will only be for a couple of weeks, right?"

"That depends on Dare Me, and how quickly he recovers. Unfortunately at his age . . ." My voice trailed away, but we both knew what I'd left unsaid. Even horses far younger than mine didn't always bounce right back from an injury. At fifteen, Dare Me's show career might well be finished.

"Of course you'll come back," Bitsy declared. "I couldn't stand it if you didn't. Who else could I share a room with?"

"Gee, I don't know. That's a tough one. How many other people do you think could put up with you?"

"Not many." As always in times of stress, her Southern drawl was even more pronounced. "Who else is going to wake me up in the morning? Or listen when I talk about my mama? Or give me advice about my love life?"

"Speaking of your love life, how are things going with you and Tommy?"

"Pretty well."

"Come on," I said. "Give. What's the matter?"

"Compared with what's happened to you, I guess I really don't have any right to complain. It's just that ... well, in the beginning I had sort of a crush on Tommy, you know?"

"Do I ever!"

"I know you were always saying that the only other person who thought Tommy was so great was Tommy himself, but I never believed that for a minute. I was sure that behind that loud, show-off exterior was a really sensitive boy. The only problem is that . . ."

"Behind the loud, show-off exterior, you found a loud, show-off of a boy," I finished for her.

"He's not that bad! Well I guess sometimes he is. Isn't that awful?"

"Not at all. We all make mistakes. Besides, I'd say you're doing pretty well if the only thing you did wrong was to give someone more credit than he deserved."

"But now I feel like such a dope. Tommy seems to like me, and I don't have the heart to try and cool things off."

"That's the problem with you Southern belles. You're too soft. Do you think that if Tommy was tired of you, he'd make any bones about breaking it off?"

Bitsy looked horrified. "It's not that I'm tired of him!" she said correcting me. "What a terrible way to put things! I still like Tommy. It's just that I'd rather have him for a friend, than a boyfriend, if you see what I mean. I just don't think we're suited to each other that way."

"No sparks, huh?"

"More like a fizzle. Do you think I'm doing something wrong?"

"Of course not. You've just got the wrong boy, that's all."

"My mama always told me that when the right boy came along, I'd know it."

"Everybody's mother always told them that. It must be in the first chapter of the motherhood manual or something."

"But then along came Tommy, and I thought he was the one. How am I ever going to be able to trust my judgment after that?"

"So he wasn't Mr. Right. He wasn't Mr. Totally Wrong either. Admit it, you have had some good times this summer."

"Well of course I have. But it wasn't just because of Tommy. There was you, and Josh..." Bitsy stopped, her eyes misted again. "Oh, Alex, what am I going to do when you go home? Nothing will be the same!"

"Sure it will," I said. But deep down inside I was thinking the very same thing myself.

Chapter Eight

The next morning, I went over to the show ground early to talk to Jack.

"He was here a couple of minutes ago," Pete told me. "I guess he'll be back soon." He peered at me closely. "You don't look too good," he said in an uncommon show of brotherly concern. "Do you want to sit down or something?"

"No, I'll be all right." I walked down the aisle to Dare Me's stall.

The gelding had finished eating. He looked around expectantly as I appeared in his doorway, and I wondered if he remembered our early-morning rides, and missed them as keenly as I did. He ambled over and pushed his muzzle into my hand, blowing softly and leaning against the canvas webbing stall guard as though trying to push his way out.

Well why not? Just because he was too sore to be ridden didn't mean he might not enjoy a walk. Picking up the halter that hung from a nail beside his stall, I slipped it over his head, then fastened the leather strap beneath his throat.

Dare Me pricked his ears eagerly, pulling at the lead rope as we reached the end of the aisle and he saw the empty field that opened out before me. He'd spent the last four days standing in his stall with a poultice on his leg, and I couldn't blame him for feeling itchy. Necessary though the rest was, it was hard on his Thoroughbred soul to be confined.

He arched his neck, craning his head one way then the other to look around the field. I could understand his feelings. He'd been a show horse for a long time, and he loved the life—the excitement, the competition, the glory—every bit as much as I did. It wasn't going to be any easier for him to give it up than it was for me.

We spent over an hour walking around the show ground, and by the time we'd finished, it was no longer empty. A steady stream of cars was winding its way in the entrance as the exhibitors arrived in their crisp britches and their polished boots, to get ready for the day's competition ahead. Looking down at my faded jeans and scuffed sneakers, I was acutely aware of the chasm that had opened up between us. I belonged, but I didn't belong. The other riders' concerns, their hopes, their dreams, which only days before had been tightly intertwined with my own, now had nothing to do with me at all.

Walking back to the stable area, I passed by the cafeteria tent, which was now doing a bustling business in hot coffee, dry eggs and greasy sausages. To my surprise, I saw Josh, Tommy and Bitsy seated at one of the outside tables, talking to one another animatedly.

What was Bitsy doing here so early? I wondered. Since she didn't have a class until afternoon, I knew nothing short of a national emergency could have gotten her out of bed at eight o'clock. My curiosity aroused, I steered Dare Me in their direction.

They were so engrossed in their conversation, they didn't even see me approach until I was almost upon them. Then Tommy looked up and cleared his throat loudly. Immediately, all conversation stopped.

I felt curiously left out. It was as though they, too, shared my feeling that I was already an outsider, someone who was no longer to be considered a part of what they were doing.

"Oh, hi, Alex," said Bitsy. She flashed me a bright smile. "Would you like to join us?"

"I don't think so." I gestured toward Dare Me who was waiting patiently behind me. "He wouldn't fit at the table." Nobody laughed at my feeble attempt at a joke. Was it my imagination, I wondered, or did they actually look relieved that I wouldn't be able to stay?

"Well, I guess I'd better be getting him back to his stall."

"You do that," Josh advised, and I got the uncomfortable impression that I was being shooed away.

"See you around," Tommy called after me as I walked away. I couldn't help noticing that as soon as I was out of earshot, their conversation started right back up again.

Probably I was just being paranoid. Those people were my friends, my best friends. I just couldn't believe that just because I wasn't going to be riding on the circuit with them anymore, they wouldn't want anything to do with me.

Later that morning, a horse and rider fell during the Grand Prix preliminaries they were holding in the main ring. The rider was fine, but the horse had broken his leg in two places and had to be destroyed. That type of thing didn't happen often, but when it did, the whole day went out of whack.

With all the commotion going on, I didn't get a chance to speak to Jack until afternoon.

"Oh, good, Al, you're here. I've been meaning to talk to you." Jack waved me alongside as he hurried a working hunter up to the outside course where a professional rider was waiting to take over.

"It's about Dare Me," I began, taking two steps for every one of his. For a short man, he could move surprisingly fast. "I've made my decision."

Jack nodded. "That's what I wanted to talk to you about. I spoke with Josh earlier..."

Why Josh?

"And he told me about the plan the four of you have hatched up. Actually, asked my permission, is more like it. I wanted to talk to you alone first before we brought the others into it. I don't mind telling you this is a risky thing to do—not for you particularly, you've got no choice. But for the other three—"

"Jack wait! What on earth are you talking about?"

"You mean you haven't spoken to Josh?"

"Except for early this morning, I haven't seen him all day."

Jack muttered something under his breath which I knew I was better off not trying to decipher.

"Look," he said, "I don't have time to explain the whole thing now. If I don't get this horse up to the outside course right away, he's going to miss his class. Go find Josh, and talk to him. When the working class is over, I'll want to see all four of you back at the tack room. Got it?"

"Got it!" What in the world was going on?

I hurried off in the direction of the barns to find Josh. I found him sitting in the tack room, applying a coat of polish to his muddy boots.

I hesitated in the doorway. "What's up?" I asked. "Jack said a few odd things, then told me to come and find you."

"Odd how?" Josh asked. He gave me a friendly look and a wave of relief washed over me. Obviously he'd decided not to hold yesterday's outburst against me.

"You know, strange. They didn't make any sense. Something about there not being much risk for me, but I should think about what it might do to the rest of you." I shot him a perplexed glance. "I didn't have the slightest idea what he was talking about. He seemed to think you might."

"I do. I talked it over this morning with Tommy and Bitsy, and they said it was all right with them, so then I went to Jack. I was getting around to you next."

"Why am I always the last to know anything?" I complained. "So what exactly is it that I don't know?"

Josh laid aside the tin of polish, picked up a brush and attacked his boots fiercely. I got the distinct impression that he didn't quite want to meet my eye. "Well," he began, "after yesterday, I was pretty sure that you were going to send Dare Me home from the circuit."

I stared at him, openmouthed. It's disconcerting to have a boy understand you better than you understand yourself.

"Then this morning, I spoke with Bitsy and she told me it was true. For the past few days, I'd kind of been toying with an idea, but I didn't want to say anything about it until I knew for sure what you were going to do."

"Okay," I said, still no more enlightened than I'd been at the beginning. "Go on."

"You see, it occurred to me that sending Dare Me home from the circuit and sending you home were not necessarily one and the same thing—"

"Sure they are," I broke in. "What good does it do me to go on to the shows if I'm not going to be able to ride in them?"

"That's just my point," said Josh. "You can't ride Dare Me, but that doesn't mean you can't show another horse."

The light was beginning to dawn. "You mean, for example," I said slowly, scarcely daring to hope, "like China Doll?"

"Precisely. Or Lobo, or Blithe Spirit, for that matter."

"You're kidding!" I cried. "You guys would do that for me?"

Josh nodded. "We got together and talked things over this morning. The way we figure it, you've already got two Medals, and two Maclays, so we're really only talking about one more of each. I'm already qualified for the Medal, so that frees the Doll for that class. Tommy's qualified for Maclay, and he's offered to loan you Lobo. Bitsy knows what a handful Lobo can be. So, if it will makes things any easier for you, she offered to switch off with Blithe Spirit."

"I can't believe it. You guys are too much!"

"It was nothing," said Josh. If I hadn't known better I'd have sworn he was blushing. "After all the trouble you've had this summer, we figured it was the least we could do."

"Josh Connelly, you're terrific!" Without even stopping to think about what I was doing, I threw myself into his arms. He pulled me to him and hugged me close.

"Ahem!" said a loud voice from behind us. "Are we interrupting something?"

I straightened quickly then looked around. Tommy was standing in the tack room, with Bitsy hovering uncertainly behind him. "No, of course not. Come on in." Moving self-consciously away from Josh, I took a seat on the other side of the room. "As a matter of fact, I was just going to come and find you. Jack said he wants to speak to us here as soon as the working class ends on the outside course."

"He must have told you our news," Bitsy said. Since my face felt like it was glowing like a neon sign, the guess wasn't a hard one to make. "So what do you think of the idea?"

"I think it's fantastic! You guys are great! I can't believe you'd actually do this for me."

"As soon as Josh explained what he had in mind, we all went for the idea in a minute," Bitsy said. "I don't know why I didn't think of it sooner. Just because Dare Me's going home, doesn't mean it has to be the end of the world. After all, like my mama always says, when you don't have a Cadillac, a Ford will do."

"Besides," said Tommy, "look at it this way. Josh and I are really only protecting our own interests. If you'd had to default, how would we ever have won our bet?"

"Bet, nothing!" I told them happily. "If you manage to see me through this, as soon as we get to

New York, I'll buy all three of you the best dinner the city has to offer.''

"You heard her!" Tommy crowed. "Four Seasons, here we come!''

"You do realize," said Josh on a more serious note, "that this only works if Dare Me is back in action in time for the finals. Assuming we all qualify, there won't be any spare horses in New York or Harrisburg.''

"Don't worry," I said, too happy to let anything spoil my mood. "He will be, I'm sure of it. With eight solid weeks of rest back at the farm, how can he help but get better?''

"You!" I said to Bitsy, when Josh got up and he and Tommy took a walk out to the end of the aisle to look for Jack. "Why didn't you tell me this was what the three of you were cooking up?''

"I didn't know," said Bitsy. "Honestly. It was all Josh's idea. The first Tommy and I heard of it was this morning when he called and said I had to get right over to the show grounds for an emergency meeting. That's what we were discussing over at the cafeteria when you came by.''

"I was wondering what could have gotten you out of bed at the crack of dawn.''

"Well, Josh said it was important, and that it concerned you, so of course I came.''

"You guys are terrific," I said, my voice ending in a loud sniffle.

Jack chose that moment to appear. "Oh for Pete's sake, Alex, don't go all watery on us," he said crossly. "We've got work to do. I told you to round up four bodies." He looked around the small room. "What's the matter? I only see two."

"They're right outside." I ducked past him and used the moment it took to round up Josh and Tommy to compose myself. By the time we were all seated in the tack room, I was ready for anything.

"All right, then," said Jack, looking at each one of us in turn. "There aren't many kids who would put their own chances of winning on the line in order to help out a friend. I guess what I'm trying to say is that your parents must have raised you right, and Alex here should be darn grateful for that fact."

"Yes, Jack," we chorused together. We'd been responding that way for so long, we didn't even stop to think about whether it was appropriate or not.

"Now, let's get down to brass tacks. I want each and every one of you to know exactly what you're getting into. Josh—right now, you're in the best shape. You've got all your Medals and two Maclays, which means that Alex will probably be riding China Doll more than anyone else. Her style is totally different from yours. Have you stopped to think how switching off riders might affect the mare's performance in the jumper classes? You're currently leading for the high score award, you know."

"Yes," said Josh. "I know. It's a risk I'm willing to take."

"Tommy." Jack went to the next one of us in turn. "You still need two Maclays, and Lobo's been fighting you all the way. We both know that he'd rather tackle the jumper courses. To tell the truth, you're lucky if that horse has enough patience for one equitation class a day, much less two. Have you considered how you might feel if Alex rides him in the Maclay earlier, and then he blows up later with you in the Medal?"

"Don't worry about Lobo," Tommy said confidently. "I can handle him."

Jack did not look entirely convinced, but he continued down the line, concentrating on Bitsy. "You," he said, "have got the most to lose. You're still three wins short of qualifying for both shows. Normally, this time of year, I'd say that's no problem. But you better realize that for every show you give up Blithe Spirit and take in a horse you have very little previous experience on, you're cutting your chances of winning in half."

"I agree with Josh," Bitsy said firmly, and I could have kissed her. Come to think of it, I could have kissed all four of them. "That's just a chance we'll have to take."

"And as for you," said Jack, his eyes resting finally on me. "Winning's tough enough in this kind of competition. What makes you think you have any chance at all of beating all those other kids riding a bunch of horses you've never even been on before?"

"It's more of a chance than I'll have if I don't try," I said. Listening to him go down the line had made me fully aware of just how big a risk my friends had been willing to take for my sake. How would I ever be able to repay their generosity?

"All right. Just so long as you know what you're getting into." He looked around at the four of us and for a moment, I swear, his expression softened. Then the moment was gone, and he was his old self again as he turned and headed for the door.

"By the way, only a fool would think he could climb on somebody's horse cold and expect to win. Anybody here thinks they might need an extra lesson or two, I'm available." His gaze, as it swept around the room, was meaningful. "I'm sure your mothers didn't raise any fools."

Chapter Nine

The next morning, I said goodbye to Dare Me and he was loaded onto a van to be shipped home. Then the rest of us moved to C.W. Post, a college on the western end of Long Island, where the next week's show was to take place.

"Guess what?" said Bitsy in the car on the way up. "I had a long talk with Tommy last night, and we agreed that maybe it's better if we start seeing a bit less of each other."

"You both agreed? Or was that how you told him it was going to be?"

"No, honestly. Scout's honor, it was a mutual decision."

"Don't hand me that. You were never a girl scout and I know it."

"All right, then, on my honor as a member of the Atlanta chapter of the Daughters of the Civil War."

"There isn't really such a thing, is there?"

"Of course. We meet monthly to reminisce about the good old days when the South was in its glory." Her voice took on a solemn note. "When men were gentlemen, and women were ladies—"

"Never mind all that. Just tell me everything that you said to Tommy."

"It wasn't really that big a deal. We both agreed it was probably better to cool things off for a while. I mean, when you stop to consider that in the six weeks we've been going together, we've seen one another almost every day, well, that's really pretty intense."

"I see your point. In normal high school life, that's got to be almost a whole year's worth of dates."

"Besides," Bitsy added, "speaking of school, it's about to start up again, and I know for a fact that Tommy's worried about keeping his grades up. Between that and the pressure we're under to qualify, neither one of us is going to be having a whole lot of spare time."

"So you decided just to be friends instead?"

"Sort of like you and Josh."

"Yes, well . . ." I said, blushing. "Then I'm sure you'll do just fine."

"Like you and Josh are?" Bitsy prompted. She never was one to leave well enough alone.

"Exactly," I said.

"So," she said, digging around with all the fervor of a mole in topsoil. "You two seemed to be such good buddies yesterday in the tack room, why aren't you going out?"

"What you saw," I told her firmly, "was a spontaneous gesture of affection between friends. And," I added after a moment's pause, "the reason we aren't going out is that Josh hasn't asked me to."

"Hasn't asked you to?" Bitsy shrieked. The sound bounced off the walls of the car's small interior. "He spent half the summer following you around."

"That was different."

"Different how?"

"Then he was only doing it so that he and Tommy wouldn't have to split up. You know, so that the four of us could go places together."

"In a pig's eye!" It was the closest I'd ever heard Bitsy come to swearing. "Tommy told me Josh really likes you."

"Tommy doesn't know his head from a hole in the wall."

"Sometimes I think you're the one with air where your brain ought to be. I don't know why you can't see what's sitting right in front of your face."

"Oh sure," I said sarcastically. "I suppose just because we spend more time fighting than we do anything else, is no reason to think that we don't get along. Do you realize that the only time we've ever been out together, just the two of us, was a spur-of-the-moment visit to a country fair? That's not exactly my idea of a hot and heavy romance."

"You haven't exactly given Josh the easiest time of it this summer. Has it ever occurred to you, though, that maybe he's waiting for you to indicate a little interest in him before he pulls out all the stops?"

"Not really," I answered, "maybe it's like you and Tommy. He'd rather be friends, and he isn't planning on pulling them out at all."

At C.W. Post, we got a first-hand view of the problems Jack had been talking about. When it was time for the Medal, Josh lent me China Doll, his huge, black mare, who was nothing like Dare Me at all. Despite the extra lesson Jack managed to squeeze in, by the time we entered the ring, I still felt more like a crane operator than an equestrian. Needless to say, we didn't make the call-backs.

When the Maclay came, I climbed aboard Lobo. By now, I was feeling slightly less optimistic about our plan than I had at the beginning, and Tommy's headstrong gelding did nothing to dispel my doubts. That he was used to a firmer hand at the helm became obvious when we scored the fastest trip in the history of the class.

"Whew," said Bitsy. She gave me a sympathetic smile as I came out of the ring. "He really took you for a ride."

"I know. It's a shame we're not at Aqueduct. The way he was going, I probably could have won there."

"Too bad," said Tommy, taking the gelding's reins as I slid off. "But I did tell you he likes to gallop on."

What he'd neglected to mention was that the horse had a mouth like concrete and a brain to match.

"Don't worry," said Josh, flashing me a jaunty "thumbs up." "This is only the beginning. Things are bound to get better from here on in."

They'd have to, I thought. They couldn't get much worse.

Though I did poorly, the week was not a total loss. Bitsy won her second Medal on Blithe Spirit;

and once again, Josh captured the Junior Jumper Championship with China Doll. When Saturday night rolled around, they were in a mood for celebrating.

"We're all going out to a movie," said Bitsy. "Want to join us?"

"Why not? It sounds like fun."

We chose a comedy that none of us had seen, which wasn't hard to do considering that we'd been on the road together all summer. When we reached the movie theater, Josh and I stopped to buy popcorn while Tommy and Bitsy went on ahead to save some seats. I ended up sitting next to Josh, with Tommy on my other side.

I have to say one thing for Tommy. He really knows how to enjoy a movie. As time went on, his laughter got louder and louder, finally turning into genuine guffaws that seemed to fill the entire theatre.

I kept moving farther and farther over in my seat, trying to pretend that I wasn't with him. I didn't dare look at Bitsy on the other side, but I'd have bet anything that she was doing the same thing.

By the time the plot was beginning to wind down, I was almost sitting in Josh's lap. If not for the armrest that separated us, I probably would have been. He didn't seem to mind though. At one point when the screen was full of shadows and the theater around us darkened, he reached over and took my hand.

When the house lights came on as the credits began to roll, he was still holding on. "What do you guys say to a burger?" he asked Tommy and Bitsy, as though my answer was already assured. "Ali and I are starved."

For a brief moment, it crossed my mind to protest his high-handed manner, but the truth of the matter was, I really was hungry. We found a burger joint that was still open, then spent most of the meal rehashing the movie we had just seen. It was almost midnight by the time we got back to the motel.

"That was great," said Bitsy, stifling a wide yawn. She unlocked the door and let herself into our room. "But now I'm so tired, I can't wait to get into bed."

"Me too," said Tommy, sauntering away in the direction of the other wing where their room was located.

Josh and I were left by ourselves in the deserted hallway. "Well," I said, smiling uncertainly. "That was fun. But I guess I better be going—"

I began to back away, but Josh took my hand and pulled me toward him. "Why are you always putting me off, Ali?"

"I'm not."

Instead of arguing, Josh simply held on to my hand, his dark eyes staring down into mine. Was he going to kiss me? Was I going to kiss him?

I'd never kissed a boy before. Traveling around as much as I did, when would I get the chance? Of course, I suppose you could count Freddie Fergeson in the fourth grade.

"What are you thinking?" Josh asked. "You look a million miles away."

I wasn't about to tell him the truth, so instead I popped out with the first thing that came to mind. "I'm wondering why you always call me Ali. Nobody does but you."

"I know. Jack calls you Al, Bitsy calls you Alex, and Pete, when he's mad at you, calls you Alexandra."

"I've noticed. It's enough to make a person schizophrenic."

"But none of those names seemed right to me," Josh continued. "Alexandra's too formal, and Al and Alex are both boy's names. Ali just seemed to suit you."

Josh was still looking at me very intently, and I couldn't decide whether that meant he wanted to kiss me. Then he leaned toward me, and I stopped speculating.

* * *

For the next few weeks I didn't have much to cheer about. We spent the first half of September back in Connecticut and, considering how well I did in the two shows there, I might as well not have bothered.

I rode Lobo and China Doll in the first one and my results were the same as they had been the week before. Then Bitsy lent me Blithe Spirit and, though things improved, it still wasn't enough. I managed a second and a third, which was much better than I had done before, certainly, but still no help as far as qualifying was concerned.

I'd heard it said that some horses responded better to boys, and some to girls, but I'd never really believed it was true. After all, the professional riders climbed on anything that came their way, and they always seemed to make things work. Now, however, I couldn't help wondering.

It was perfectly obvious that I was much more comfortable with Bitsy's mare, Blithe Spirit, than I had been with either Lobo or China Doll. Whether they were used to longer legs, a stronger hand, or just more weight in the saddle, neither of the guys' horses was nearly as responsive to my aids as Blithe. Which was unfortunate because while Josh managed to pick up his third Maclay at the Fairfield fall show, which meant he was now fully qualified; Bitsy and I still each needed one win in each class.

In mid-September we moved back down to Long Island for two shows there, and that's when my luck finally began to change. At North Shore, Bitsy lent me Blithe Spirit and I won the Medal class which meant I was now qualified for the finals at the Pennsylvania National Horse Show in Harrisburg. Then, riding China Doll, I pulled a third in the Maclay—not perfect by any means, but certainly a step in the right direction.

Elated as I was by my results, I couldn't help but notice that Bitsy, after congratulating me briefly, made herself scarce. In fact, if I hadn't known better, I'd have sworn as the week wore on, that she was avoiding me. Did she resent the fact that I had won the Medal and she hadn't? Did she think that perhaps if she had ridden Blithe herself in the class, that she'd be the one who was now qualified? Though it wasn't necessarily true, I could certainly see how Bitsy might have come to that conclusion.

The following week at Piping Rock, my success continued. On Saturday morning, I came first in the Maclay, chalking up that last, highly coveted win.

Josh and Tommy, neither of whom had ridden in the class, were both there to share my excitement. We were all talking and laughing at once, and it was a moment before I realized that Bitsy, who had been in the ring with me, must had ridden right on past without even stopping.

"Uh-oh," I said worriedly. "She must be upset. I better go find her."

"Give her a few minutes alone," Josh advised. "It's never easy to watch someone else celebrate a win, especially when that means that you yourself just lost. I'm sure she's happy for you. She just needs a little time to realize it, that's all."

I decided to follow his advice. After seeing China Doll back to her stall, the three of us went and grabbed a burger for lunch. When, that afternoon, Tommy aced the Medal class for his last win, we nearly went wild, waving and cheering and running around the show ground with foolish grins on our faces. Anybody watching us must have thought we had lost our minds.

"Look out championships, here we come!" Tommy cried, grabbing me and swinging me around the tack room in an impromtu dance as Josh watched with a big grin. "I can't believe it's finally done!"

"I know what you mean," I agreed. Though it had only really been four months, it had seemed to take forever.

"All I can say," Josh added, "is that it's about time. Do you realize that with the show in Harrisburg starting October 10th, there are only two more weekends left to qualify? That's what I call taking it down to the wire.''

"Well you know my motto," Tommy said lightly. "Never do today what you can put off till tomorrow."

"Seriously," I said looking back and forth between them. "I want to thank you both. You know I never would have gotten this far without you. A month ago, I was ready to pack it in and go home. If it hadn't been for you guys and Bitsy..." My voice trailed away as the same thought hit all three of us at the same time.

Where was Bitsy? Except during our classes, none of us had seen her all day. We'd all been so wrapped up in celebrating our own good fortune that none of us had even really noticed she was gone!

"Are you thinking what I'm thinking?" Josh asked.

"She still needs one of each," I said. "Or she won't be going anywhere."

"Two more wins, and only two shows to get them in," Tommy said sympathetically. "That's going to be rough."

"Rough isn't the word for it," Josh said, voicing an opinion we all shared. "Unless everything falls her way."

"Then we'll just have to make sure that everything does, won't we?" I said.

"You said it," Josh cried, and Tommy nodded. "Let's go find her."

But Bitsy was nowhere to be found.

Chapter Ten

W here in the world have you been?'' I screamed, slamming the motel door behind me.

It was six o'clock that evening and Bitsy was sitting in the middle of her bed calmly munching on an apple. We'd been looking for her for three hours and I was really beginning to get worried.

"Josh and Tommy and I have been going crazy looking for you!"

"I've been right here," Bitsy said coolly, as though there was nothing at all unusual about her leaving the show in the middle of the day. "I felt a little tired so I decided to come back and take a nap."

Now I knew something was wrong. Bitsy might be one of the world's great all-time sleepers, but she never took naps in the afternoon. "How did you get back here? I thought you were going to catch a ride with me."

"Mary Lou Nelson had forgotten her spurs and had to make a quick trip back so I tagged along with her."

"I see." I didn't see at all. I knew Bitsy had to be disappointed that she hadn't done better at the show, but by this time we were all used to the circuit having its ups and downs. Why was she acting so strangely?

Now that I thought about it, she and I hadn't been nearly as tight as usual for the last couple of weeks. I'd been so caught up with trying to ride strange horses and taking extra lessons from Jack, that I hadn't really had the time to think about Bitsy.

Bitsy and I had been friends for four years, and in that time we'd been more places and done more things than most friends do in a lifetime. We'd shared a room, but that was only the beginning. More importantly, we'd shared our hopes and our dreams. We'd kept each other's secrets and laughed at each other's silly jokes. If something was wrong between us now, I wanted to know what it was.

"Do you feel okay?" I asked cautiously.

"I never said I wasn't feeling well. I was just a little tired, that's all!"

"Okay, okay. You don't have to snap my head off."

"Sorry. You realize Josh and Tommy won the bet today, don't you?" she asked.

"I thought we called that bet off a month ago, when you three guys offered to help me out. I said I was going to take everybody out to dinner myself when we all got to New York, remember?"

"*If* we all get to New York," Bitsy said meaningfully.

Realization dawned. I should have known what the problem was. Now that the other three of us were qualified, Bitsy was nervous, and justifiably so, that she might never make it to the finals at all.

"I was looking for you earlier," I said. "I wanted to thank you for letting me ride Blithe. You know I never could have qualified without her."

"You're welcome."

"And I just wanted to let you know that Josh and Tommy and I are sure you're going to make it, too. We're all pulling for you a hundred percent, and if there's anything we can do to help—"

"Oh for Pete's sake, how do you expect me to stay mad when you're going out of your way to be so nice?"

I crossed the room and sat down on the edge of her bed. "Now, suppose you tell me what you're so mad about."

"I guess I'm not really mad, exactly. It's more that I'm worried."

"I would be, too," I admitted honestly. "Actually I've been pretty much of a basket case this last month because I was so afraid I wouldn't make it."

"You? Cool-as-a-Cucumber Anderson? I don't believe it!"

"Ah come on. You know me better than that. The more nervous I am, the more I hold things inside."

"I suppose so. Although it hasn't seemed like that at all. Even when you were riding that crazy Lobo, you never looked anything less than totally confident. That's why it really freaked me out to see you on Blithe. I'd watch you lay down a really solid trip and I'd be jealous, because it seemed as though she'd never gone nearly so well for me."

"How could you be jealous? It was all the work that you've put into training Blithe that made me look good. She virtually shows herself."

"She's not quite a push button," Bitsy demurred, but I could tell she was pleased.

"Tell me something, and be honest, because I really want to know. Were you mad at me last week when I won the Medal on Blithe and you were stuck with China Doll?"

"Maybe a little," Bitsy admitted. "But only at first. As soon as I had a chance to think about it, I realized that the judges picked your performance, not the horse's. Blithe may have made things easier, but she didn't win the blue ribbon for you."

"Since we're being honest, I have to confess I've been feeling pretty bad myself. Every time I borrowed Blithe from you and then didn't win, I wondered if maybe I had taken away a chance that you might have had to qualify. I really feel like my making it to the finals is a joint effort. It won't mean anything to me at all if you're not there, too."

"Believe me," Bitsy said fervently. "I intend to try my best."

I felt much better now that we were on the same side, rather than working against one another. "So," I said teasingly, "are we through fighting?"

"Fighting, huh!" Bitsy snorted. "You Yankees sure do know how to blow things out of proportion. Why this was nothing more than a little spat. It's like my mama always says, 'If you can't get mad at people, then they aren't really your friends.'"

By the following weekend I was on pins and needles, and Josh and Tommy seemed equally nervous.

When Bitsy made the call-back in the Medal on Saturday, the three of us were hanging over the In gate holding our breaths. I swear it's a hundred times easier to ride the course yourself than to have to stand by helplessly while someone you really care about does it instead.

Showing no signs of the pressure, Bitsy rode Blithe to a near flawless round. When her number was called out on top, our screams were enough to spook two horses and gather a collection of dirty looks from the spectators who lined the rail. We didn't care. One win down, and only one to go.

Unfortunately, Bitsy wasn't able to repeat her performance in the Maclay later that afternoon. She was good, but not great, and had to settle for third. Still and all, we were pretty pleased. Even Jack came over and got in a word or two.

"You kids ever make spectacles of yourselves screaming at ringside like that again, and I'll have your hides," he threatened.

He patted Bitsy on the shoulder. "Nice going, Scarlet," he said, using the pet name he'd dubbed her several years earlier. "You better shine up your subway tokens. One more trip like that and you're on your way to New York."

To celebrate, we all went out to dinner. "You know," said Bitsy, when we were in our room getting changed. "It seems as though we've spent an awful lot of time this summer celebrating one thing or another by getting together with Tommy and Josh."

"It does, doesn't it? Do you think maybe they're just using us as an excuse to get a couple of gorgeous girls like us to go out with them?"

"Could be."

"You know, Josh really is pretty cute," I said.

"It's about time you noticed!"

"Oh, I've noticed all right."

"Well, when are you going to do something about it?"

"Like what?"

"Like stop holding him at arm's length. Like start giving him a chance."

"I have been. Haven't I?"

"Let's just say you haven't been obviously encouraging him. Maybe it's like you said before when we were talking about riding. The more something means to you, the more you hold it inside."

What Bitsy said was interesting. I'd never quite thought of things that way before, and now I wanted to stop and explore my feelings to try and figure out if she was right. But at that moment the boys arrived, and any chance I might have had for quiet introspection was gone.

The next week was a long one. Since the equitation classes weren't going to be held until the weekend, we had six days to wait before finding out whether Bitsy was going to make it or not. In the meantime, Josh and Tommy were showing in the jumper classes, and Bitsy had Blithe in junior hunters, but I was only marking time.

On Friday night I got some good news when Jack unexpectedly sought me out. "I talked to Rich last night," he said as he propped his foot on the rail to lean on the fence beside me.

Rich, I knew, was his stable manager at home while Jack was on the road.

"He said your gelding's doing just fine. Heat's gone, swelling's down and they've started him on some light work. As long as you don't expect too much too soon, I don't see any reason why he shouldn't be ready in time for the finals. I told Rich that unless something comes up, he should put him on the van in two weeks and ship him straight to Harrisburg, and we'll meet him there."

"Oh Jack!" I cried. "Thank you!"

"Don't thank me. I didn't do anything. It's that horse of yours. He wanted to come back, and he did. You want to thank someone, talk to his ancestors. He didn't come by that Thoroughbred spirit by accident, you know."

"Yes, Jack." I answered meekly.

"Now," he added under his breath, almost as though he was talking to himself, "if we can just get Scarlet fixed up..."

I wasn't really sure if he was talking to me or not, but I couldn't resist asking. "What do you think her chances are of winning the Medal on Saturday?"

Jack shrugged. "With so many of the kids already qualified and out of it, she's easily the best rider here. I know it, and she knows it. She's never been as strong on motivation as some of you other kids..." He paused, then looked at me and grinned. For the first time, I sensed, he was seeing me as a person, and not just one of his students. "I never told you why I took you on, did I?"

I shook my head.

"I'd seen you ride before, but last year at the Garden you were something else. Talk about feisty! You looked like you were either going to win, or die trying. I like that kind of attitude in my kids." He reached out and put a hand on my shoulder. "See if you can lend some of that determination of yours to Bitsy. She's going to need all the help she can get."

Jack's words were still running through my mind that evening back at the motel. I stopped at the soda machine to buy a drink as I pondered what he'd said. I wanted to help Bitsy any way I could.

"Hi."

Josh had come up behind me so suddenly I hadn't even heard him approach. Now I spun around in surprise and dropped my cold soda on his foot.

"That's some greeting," he said, reaching down to pick up the can. "Should I take that to mean you aren't glad to see me?"

"Sorry...yes...no! I just had my mind on other things."

Josh replaced the soda back in my hand. "I'd let that settle for a few minutes before I tried to open it," he advised. "Now then, what could possibly be so compelling to have you that deep in thought?"

"I'm worried about Bitsy," I said. There was a flight of stairs next to the soda machine, and I sank down onto the bottom one.

"We're all worried about Bitsy," Josh replied, sitting down beside me. "Come on, what gives?"

"I just have this feeling that if she doesn't qualify tomorrow, it'll be all my fault."

"Your fault? Don't you think you're taking things a bit personally?"

"Not at all. What about those times she lent me Blithe and had to make do with somebody else? Maybe if she hadn't been so generous, or if I hadn't been so selfish, she'd be on her way to the finals right now."

"Then again," Josh pointed out. "Maybe she wouldn't. The two of you have two completely different riding styles, you know. Some judges like one. Others will prefer the other. When you won, it was because you gave the best ride of the day, for a judge who liked what you had to offer. It's not as though you kept Bitsy out of the ring entirely. She was there, but you rode better, it's as simple as that."

"Maybe the reason I rode better was because I was riding her horse."

"That's the key to this whole thing right there," Josh said. "You were riding a borrowed horse, just as Bitsy was. Your riding Blithe wasn't what kept Bitsy from winning. Your beating her, fair and square, was."

"You're right," I said, smiling at him. Our eyes met. For a moment my breath caught in my throat. "Well," I said quickly, starting to rise. "I'd better be going..."

"What's your hurry?" Josh took my arm and held it.

"Bitsy's expecting me."

"She won't be worried. She knows you're with me. I stopped by your room before, that's how I knew where to find you."

"You did?"

"Mm-hm." Josh nodded. "I wanted to see you tonight."

"I can't. I told Bitsy I'd—"

"I dare you," Josh said softly.

"You've done that to me before, Josh Connelly."

"Yes, I have. And as I recall, it worked out okay. Since this is the second time, I guess maybe I ought to double dare you."

"All right." I grinned at him. "What is it this time?"

Josh's smile was slow and satisfied. "I dare you not to keep running away from me, Ali."

My first impulse was to deny it. Then I remembered what Bitsy and I had discussed. Maybe I had been putting Josh off, the way she'd said.

Which wasn't to say that I was going to make things easy for him. Instead, I threw back his challenge with one of my own. "I'm not running now, Josh."

Can I help it if I'm a sucker for a well-placed dimple? The next thing I knew Josh was kissing me.

"Now that we've got that settled," said Josh after a while. "What do you say we go give Bitsy some moral support?"

"Settled, huh!" I snorted as he draped his arm over my shoulder and we started down the hall. "I have no intention of settling down for anybody."

"Good," said Josh. "That's exactly the way I like it."

The next afternoon Bitsy's cheering section was the most ardent trio of supporters north of the Mason-Dixon line. As she was standing at the In gate, waiting for her turn in the ring, I whipped a rag out of the back pocket of a passing groom and gave her boots one last polish for luck.

"Go get 'em," I told her. "You know what your mama always says, 'It takes a hundred Yankees to whip one good ole Southern gal.'"

"My mama never said that!"

"She didn't? Well maybe she should have, because it's true. Now go out there and ride that course as though you mean it!"

The gate swung open before her, and Bitsy rode Blithe into the ring. There are a lot of things I like about Bitsy, but that day the thing I liked the best was that she really knew how to pull through in a pinch. She rode the course as though her life depended on it.

When she made the call-backs, we were right there, gripping each other for support as we hung anxiously over the rail. Even Jack was not immune to the pressure. Pacing back and forth in the warm-up area, he muttered and swore under his breath, counting strides and judging distances and riding every step of the way with her.

Mindful of his reaction the week before, we steeled ourselves not to scream when the results were announced. Which is why, when Bitsy's number was called for the blue ribbon, the loudest sound on the show ground was the triumphant war whoop that came from the short, bushy-haired man pacing outside the ring. Then, as if there'd been nothing unusual about his reaction, Jack hurried off to the outside course.

Bitsy emerged from the ring, clutching the precious blue ribbon in her hands. There was a huge grin on her face and tears running down her cheeks, which, I figured, summed the whole thing up pretty well. We all ran to congratulate her.

"We did it!" We cried in unison, laughing and hugging each other. "We did it.

"New York. Here we come!"

First Love from Silhouette

READERS' COMMENTS

"Before reading your books I felt that reading was a bore and a plain waste of time. Well, your terrific books proved me wrong. Thanks a lot!"
—*K.A., New York, N.Y.*

"I'd just like to say that you're doing a great job. I know I should reserve one book for each week of the month, but most of the time I read a book a day because I just can't put it down."
—*E.D., Riverside, CA*

"I had never read a First Love until my mother brought one home for me. I liked it so much that I gave it to my girlfriend, and since then we've been reading and trading First Loves like crazy! Thanks for making your wonderful books and bringing them to all of us teens."
—*L.G., Hull, MA*

"I really love your stories. They are so real I feel I'm part of the book. The characters seem to come to life. They are my age and share some of the problems I have in my everyday life. Keep up the good work!
—*D.K., Baltimore, MD*

America's Favorite Teenage Romance

QUANTITY	BOOK #	ISBN #	TITLE	AUTHOR	PRICE
☐	129	06129-3	The Ghost of Gamma Rho	Elaine Harper	$1.95
☐	130	06130-7	Nightshade	Jesse Osborne	1.95
☐	131	06131-5	Waiting for Amanda	Cheryl Zach	1.95
☐	132	06132-3	The Candy Papers	Helen Cavanagh	1.95
☐	133	06133-1	Manhattan Melody	Marilyn Youngblood	1.95
☐	134	06134-X	Killebrew's Daughter	Janice Harrell	1.95
☐	135	06135-8	Bid for Romance	Dorothy Francis	1.95
☐	136	06136-6	The Shadow Knows	Becky Stewart	1.95
☐	137	06137-4	Lover's Lake	Elaine Harper	1.95
☐	138	06138-2	In the Money	Beverly Sommers	1.95
☐	139	06139-0	Breaking Away	Josephine Wunsch	1.95
☐	140	06140-4	What I Know About Boys	McClure Jones	1.95
☐	141	06141-2	I Love You More Than Chocolate	Frances Hurley Grimes	1.95
☐	142	06142-0	The Wilder Special	Rose Bayner	1.95
☐	143	06143-9	Hungarian Rhapsody	Marilyn Youngblood	1.95
☐	144	06144-7	Country Boy	Joyce McGill	1.95
☐	145	06145-5	Janine	Elaine Harper	1.95
☐	146	06146-3	Call Back Yesterday	Doreen Owens Malek	1.95
☐	147	06147-1	Why Me?	Beverly Sommers	1.95
☐	149	06149-8	Off the Hook	Rose Bayner	1.95
☐	150	06150-1	The Heartbreak of Haltom High	Dawn Kingsbury	1.95
☐	151	06151-X	Against the Odds	Andrea Marshall	1.95
☐	152	06152-8	On the Road Again	Miriam Morton	1.95
☐	159	06159-5	Sugar 'n' Spice	Janice Harrell	1.95
☐	160	06160-9	The Other Langley Girl	Joyce McGill	1.95

Your Order Total $ _____

☐ (Minimum 2 Book Order)
New York and Arizona residents
add appropriate sales tax $ _____

Postage and Handling   .75

I enclose   _____

Name_____

Address_____

City_____

State/Prov._____Zip/Postal Code_____